Cowboy Jake Spencer's Surefire Plan For Staying Single:

1) Avoid all women who want babies! This pretty much includes every female in New Hope, Texas.

2) Don't allow yourself to be turned by a pretty face and a pair of tight jeans, especially if the long-legged beauty is one baby-wanting Miss Priscilla Barrington.

3) No matter how desperate her situation may seem, don't invite the lady to stay at your ranch. She'll just try to win you over by cooking dinner and ironing your socks.

4) Whatever happens, don't believe for a minute that she's really going to visit the sperm bank. It's *your* baby she wants—and it's *your* hand in marriage she'll take!

Dear Reader,

Cowboys and cops...sexy men with a swagger...just the kind of guys to make your head turn. *That's* what we've got for you this month in Silhouette Desire.

The romance begins when Taggart Jones meets his match in Anne McAllister's wonderful MAN OF THE MONTH, *The Cowboy and the Kid*. This is the latest in her captivating CODE OF THE WEST miniseries. And the fun continues with Mitch Harper in *A Gift for Baby*, the next book in Raye Morgan's THE BABY SHOWER series.

Cindy Gerard has created a dynamic hero in the *very* masculine form of J. D. Hazzard in *The Bride Wore Blue*, book #1 in the NORTHERN LIGHTS BRIDES series. And if rugged rascals are your favorite, don't miss Jake Spencer in Dixie Browning's *The Baby Notion*, which is book #1 of DADDY KNOWS LAST, Silhouette's new cross-line continuity. (Next month, look for Helen R. Myers's *Baby in a Basket* as DADDY KNOWS LAST continues in Silhouette Romance!)

Gavin Cantrell is sure to weaken your knees in *Gavin's Child* by Caroline Cross, part of the delightful BACHELORS AND BABIES promotion. And Jackie Merritt—along with hero Duke Sheridan—kicks off her MADE IN MONTANA series with *Montana Fever*.

Heroes to fall in love with—and love scenes that will make your toes curl. That's what Silhouette Desire is all about. Until next month—enjoy!

All the best,

Lucia Macro

Senior Editor

Please address questions and book requests to:
Silhouette Reader Service
U.S.: 3010 Walden Ave., P.O. Box 1325, Buffalo, NY 14269
Canadian: P.O. Box 609, Fort Erie, Ont. L2A 5X3

DIXIE BROWNING
The Baby Notion

SILHOUETTE *Desire*®
Published by Silhouette Books
America's Publisher of Contemporary Romance

This one's for Curtiss Ann Matlock,
my cowboy connection.

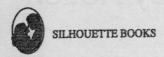 SILHOUETTE BOOKS

ISBN 0-373-76011-6

THE BABY NOTION

Copyright © 1996 by Harlequin Books S.A.

DIXIE BROWNING

has written over fifty books for Silhouette since 1980. She is a charter member of the Romance Writers of America and an award-winning author who has toured extensively for Silhouette Books. She also writes historical romances with her sister under the name Bronwyn Williams.

Meet The Soon-To-Be Moms
of New Hope, Texas!

"I'll do anything to have a baby—even if it means
going to the sperm bank. Unless sexy cowboy
Jake Spencer is willing to be a daddy...
the natural way."
—*Priscilla Barrington, hopeful mom-to-be.*

THE BABY NOTION
by Dixie Browning (Desire 7/96)

"I'm more than willing to help Mitch McCord take care
of the baby he found on his doorstep. After all, I've been
in love with that confirmed bachelor for years."
—*Jenny Stevens, maternal girl-next-door.*

BABY IN A BASKET
by Helen R. Myers (Romance 8/96)

"My soon-to-be ex-husband and I are soon-to-be
parents! Can our new arrivals also bless us with a
second chance at marriage?"
—*Valerie Kincaid, married new mom.*

MARRIED...WITH TWINS!
by Jennifer Mikels (Special Edition 9/96)

"I have vowed to be married by the time I turn thirty.
But the only man that interests me is single dad
Travis Donovan—and he doesn't know I'm alive...yet!"
—*Wendy Wilcox,
biological-clock-counting bachelorette.*

HOW TO HOOK A HUSBAND (AND A BABY)
by Carolyn Zane (Yours Truly 10/96)

"Everybody wants me to name the father of my baby.
But I can't tell anyone—even the expectant daddy!"
—*Faith Harper, prim, proper—and very pregnant.*

DISCOVERED: DADDY
by Marilyn Pappano (Intimate Moments 11/96)

One

___

Jake stepped out of the barbershop feeling naked after his long overdue haircut. Pausing on the dusty sidewalk, he pulled a list from his shirt pocket, squinted down at it and then checked off one more item. That made... let's see, florist? *Check*. Shady Grove Cemetery? *Check*. Bank? *Yep*. Barber? *Yep*. Which left the hardware store, the grocery store and—

"Hey there, Jake."

He glanced up and smiled. "Hey there, Trilla Dean."

"You going to the dance Sunday night?"

"Honey, you know me and dancing. I'd cripple half the women in New Hope if I was to show up at a dance."

"You're not all that bad."

"I'm worse, and we both know it."

She giggled. "I'll save you a dance, anyway, just in case you decide to come."

"You do that." Jake grinned and shook his head. Trilla Dean Moyers was his age. She'd put on about fifty pounds since they used to make out in the back of his truck, but with her big blue eyes and her slow, sweet smile, she didn't look a day over twenty.

Jake took out another list—Pete's grocery list, this time. Squinting some more, he muttered, "Two dove's eyes," and translated it to two dozen eggs. He didn't know which was worse—Pete's writing, or his own reading. Jake figured either his eyes were going or his arms had gotten shorter.

"Hey, Jakey."

He glanced up again and grinned at the frayed-looking redhead with two kids hanging on to her skirttails. Poor Connie. She was pregnant again. "Hey, Connie. How's Mick?"

"He's doin' better, but he's still real tore up about the Harley. I guess you heard it was totaled. Come see us sometime, y'hear?"

"I'll do that," Jake said, and meant it. Connie was another of his old classmates. They'd had a thing or two going way back in junior high school.

Jake was just about to shove the two lists back in his pocket and head over to the hardware store to see if the truck was loaded when he saw a peach-colored Cadillac convertible slide into a parking space across the street. Leaning his back against the sun-warmed brick wall, he lingered to watch the driver open the door, swing both legs out and follow them with a body that was designed to raise the noonday temperature about ten degrees.

The haystack blonde. He'd been hoping for a glimpse of her before he headed back out to the ranch. When she leaned inside the car to retrieve her purse, Jake lifted his hat and wiped the sweat off his forehead. Somebody ought to tell her, he mused, that women built the way she was built weren't cut out to wear tight jeans. Especially not when they were also wearing pink plastic sandals with four-inch heels.

Fortunately, no one ever had.

Jake flexed his shoulders, enjoying the sensation of heat on aching muscles. He didn't particularly like towns. He especially didn't like the town of New Hope, Texas. But then, he'd never been one to cut off his nose to spite his face, and catching a glimpse of his favorite fantasy always made the trip worthwhile. One of these days he was going to screw up his nerve and—

Whoa. She was fixing to go into that shop across the street.

Well, hell, as long as he was in the neighborhood...

Shrugging away from the hot brick wall, Jake rammed his lists into his pocket, carefully resettled his Stetson, and sauntered across the street, never once taking his eyes off that sweetly rounded backside.

Jake had been known to forget a name. He might even forget a face. Hell, he'd even been known to forget his own when he'd been on one of his infrequent benders. One thing he never forgot, however, was a well-turned rear end, on either a horse or a woman. He'd been seeing this particular example around town for too long now without ever getting a close look at her face.

Or maybe he just wasn't a face man.

The first time he recalled seeing her had been the day they'd auctioned off that godawful palace of old man Barringer's, along with everything in it, right down to the last solid-gold toothpick holder. Folks had come from five states to pick over the leavings.

Normally Jake wouldn't have been caught dead at a gig like that, but the old man had had a mare that Jake had wanted right bad, so he'd figured he may as well give it a shot.

And there she'd been, standing off to one side with her arms crossed and her nose in the air, like she was too good for the rest of the vultures flocking around to pick over the old bastard's carcass.

He'd got the mare, but by the time he'd wound up the paperwork, the woman had been gone. Since then he'd seen her half a dozen times, always from a distance. Sometimes she'd be walking, but mostly she'd be wheeling by in that flashy vintage Cadillac convertible. He figured she'd bought it off H. T. Barrington's estate. He'd heard the old man collected the things.

Jake didn't begrudge her the car. Right this minute he wouldn't have begrudged her every horse on his spread, and they weren't even his.

But he'd rather watch her walk than drive any day, because she had the kind of walk that would rattle every seismograph west of the Mississippi.

Jake had always liked his women a little on the wild side, slightly tacky, and strictly temporary. He figured this one might just qualify on the first two counts, what with the hair, the makeup, the tight jeans and half ton of clanking silver jewelry.

As for temporary, that could mean anything from twenty minutes to a year. Hell, even his marriage hadn't lasted a year—although the effects had lasted considerably longer.

She was talking to the store owner when he let himself inside the shop. A bell jingled softly, announcing his entrance. The sign over the door said Baby Boutique. Racks and stacks of pastel junk cluttered the place, making him feel like a bull in a china shop.

On the other hand, the sun outside was hot enough to blister paint, and the air conditioner in the china shop was going full-blast, so this bull figured he could just about handle the stress.

Feeling distinctly out of his element, Jake stepped into one of several small alcoves, this one cluttered with baby carriages and strings of plastic junk dangling from the ceiling. From where he stood, he could see the blonde's backside and the frontside of old man Harper's daughter, Faith, who owned the place. He'd met Faith once or twice—she seemed like a nice girl.

Not that Jake was interested in nice girls.

The two women were deep in conversation and Jake didn't want to barge in right off without getting a feel for the situation, so he waited for an opening. He didn't feel quite right about hanging around a female-type store, but one thing he'd learned from his rodeo days—timing was all-important.

Another thing he'd learned was that his wasn't all that great.

"...last year, or was it the year before when you spread all that money all over Shacktown?" Faith was asking as Jake quietly listened in. He thought about strolling casually over to the counter and entering into the conversation. All he needed was an opening. He could take it from there.

"How did you know about that? That was supposed to be a secret!" the blonde exclaimed.

"Honey, it was all over town before the bank even closed that day. They said you sent old Joe Sakett down to Shacktown and had him put envelopes full of money in every single mailbox."

"Oh, for heaven's sake, Faith, they weren't *full* of money. That was the year I turned twenty-seven, and I couldn't very well just hand out twenty-seven dollars to every family—I mean, that's such a piddly bunch of money. Why, I spend more than that on a pedicure.''

Pretty nice hoof-dressing, Jake mused.

''So what did you do, put in twenty-seven dollars and fifty cents? Oh, only you.''

The blonde shrugged. She had great shoulders. Funny thing—Jake had never even noticed her shoulders before.

''I added a zero, okay? Now, can we forget that so I can tell you about—''

''Oh, my God, Priss, you didn't. Two hundred and seventy dollars in *every single mailbox in Shacktown?* And by the way—putting things in people's mailboxes—isn't that a federal offense?''

''How do I know? Anyhow, nobody complained.''

Priss. Her name was Priss. Funny—she didn't look like a Priss. She looked more like a Dolly or a Wynona.

''But, Faith, what I wanted to tell you was—oh, by the way, I need a dozen teddy bears and some of those dangly things that hang over a crib. It's for my birthday celebration. And I'm not putting them in any mailboxes, so you don't have to look at me like that.''

A dozen teddy bears?

So she was celebrating a birthday. Jake could think of several ways he'd like to help her celebrate, none of which involved teddy bears.

''Anyhow,'' she continued, ''I'm not sure they'll let me put up those crib toys. They have so many gadgets and things hooked up to cribs in the hospital.''

Hospital?

Faith planted her hands on her hips. She was wearing one of those short and loose-flowing dresses. It took Jake a few minutes to realize Faith Harper was one quite *pregnant* nice girl. ''Priss,'' Faith said, ''your papa endowed the entire west wing. If anyone can talk them into it, you can."

"I wouldn't count on it. I've never been much good at throwing my weight around."

Jake sincerely begged to differ. If she got any better at it, they might both find themselves in serious trouble.

Jake cleared his throat, wanting to make his presence known but at the same time feeling like a creep for even being there. Before he could cut and run, the Harper woman spotted him, put on her professional smile and started across the room.

Jake grabbed a book off a rack, held it at arm's length and pretended to read.

"Mr. Spencer, do you need any help?"

"Who, me? Oh, um...no, thanks. Just looking. That is, one of my hands is having a baby, and—that is, his woman's having it, but—" He shrugged, giving her his best *Hey, I'm only a man, I can't help being stupid* smile and began to edge toward the door. On the way he knocked over a display of stuffed rabbits, caught three before they hit the floor and with shaking hands, began restacking the lot. The Harper woman turned back toward the counter at the back of the store, calling over her shoulder, "You just let me know when you decide, okay?"

"Yes'm, I surely will."

Jake was halfway to the door, his face on fire, when he heard the haystack blonde whisper loudly, "Who in the world is that?"

"Who, Jake? Goodness, I thought every woman in Collins County knew Jake Spencer."

So did I, Jake thought, a bit surprised. There'd been a time when he'd been downright notorious. It wasn't that long ago that he'd been living in Shacktown with his mama, working odd jobs, hustling pool and getting into trouble with the truancy officer. He'd been way ahead of Faith, and obviously the blonde, in school, but that didn't mean even they hadn't heard all the rumors about the boy who'd been every high school girl's secret dream lover and every parents' worst nightmare. If the blonde didn't remember him, she must not be a local. Either that, or she'd been off hiding under a rock when his mama died and he left town to follow the rodeo circuit—much to the pleasure of all those parents. He had ended up marrying, but the little woman had taken him for every cent he'd had and then left him laid up in a hospital in Tulsa with both legs in a cast. Guess there's no way she'd know about that, though, Jake told himself.

Jake had just about made it to the door when he made the mistake of taking one last look at the blonde. She was lifting stuffed toys down off a shelf. The first time he'd ever heard the phrase "poetry in motion" he'd thought it meant a well-trained quarter horse.

Now he knew better. She was wearing a high-necked, pink knit top that hugged her breasts and fit snugly over her body, all the way down to her concho belt. Dammit, why couldn't he just march right up there and ask her out? What the devil—she might even say yes.

It occurred to him that if he'd put in a special order, she couldn't have fit his specifications any better. A little bit wild, slightly on the tacky side, and so damned delectable he was having trouble keeping his enthusiasm down.

Right then and there Jake made up his mind that one way or another, before the summer was out, he was going to get her out of those tight jeans and into his bed. What's more, being the generous guy that he was, he'd make sure she enjoyed every minute of it just as much as he did. It wasn't like he wanted to marry her, or anything like that. God forbid!

"So anyhow," she was saying in an uppercrust Texas drawl that kind of set Jake's teeth on edge, but nowhere near enough to turn him off, "I decided that what I wanted for my birthday this year is a baby."

A baby! She was talking right out here in public about *having a baby?* Jake thought, What am I, invisible or something?

Faith opened her mouth to speak, but Priss beat her to the draw. "Oh, I know what you're going to say—it takes nine months, but, Faith, just think—your baby is due in November, and if I hurry, I could have mine by next April. Our babies can grow up together. Wouldn't that be sweet?"

"Priss, have you...who—"

"Nobody, silly, and no, I haven't, but I've been thinking about going down to the sperm bank."

With one hand on the doorknob, Jake turned back to stare. The *what* bank?

"Pricilla Joan, you wouldn't!"

Her name was Jones. Pricilla Jones. Jake decided it went with the accent.

"What in the world would you go there for?" Faith Harper demanded.

Which was exactly what Jake was wondering. He knew about New Hope's sperm bank. The day he'd first heard about it nearly five years ago—heard who had donated it to the town for the good of New Hope's future generations—he'd gone on a bender that had lasted nearly a week.

"...all alone in that big old apartment out on Willow Creek," the blonde was saying. "So I thought, why not? Everybody in town seems to be getting pregnant—mercy, I've never seen so many hatching jackets in my life. So I thought, why not me? Why can't I have a baby, too, if I want one?''

Faith took Pricilla Jones by the arm with more force than Jake would have credited her with possessing, and led the blonde over to a white wicker settee. "Sit! Now, you listen to me, Prissy. Don't you dare go and do something stupid just because Eddie ran off and married Grace Hudgins.''

Priss-Prissy-Pricilla shrugged again. It occurred to Jake, who was becoming almost as fascinated with the woman's mind as he was with her body, that she could've given lessons in body motion to a belly dancer. "Oh, him. I didn't like him all that much anyway.''

Jake thought Faith's expression looked sort of dubious and sympathetic all at the same time, which made him wonder who this Eddie guy was.

Whoever he was, he was evidently out of the picture now.

With studied casualness, Jake turned to examine a display of miniature quilts near the door. From there he had a perfect view of the blonde's profile. *Go ahead, you jerk—make the lady's acquaintance and ask her out!*

She had a high forehead under that heap of streaky blond hair that reminded him so much of the haystack he'd like to lay her down in. Her big brown eyes were set off with a thicket of lashes that looked too dark for a natural blonde, but what the hell? Her nose was a little on the short side, and even from here he could see a few freckles, but it was a real nice nose, and Jake had never even thought much about noses.

As for the rest of her...

His gaze followed the hilly route south. He hitched up his jeans, which seemed to have suddenly shrunk a couple of sizes.

It struck him that he was behaving more like a fifteen-year-old kid high on hormones than a thirty-five-year-old horse broker who ought to know better.

"I made the mistake of stopping by this morning to pick up some literature, but I forgot that Miss Agnes works there on Thursdays. Honestly, Faith, that woman has a tongue like you wouldn't believe. She looks so sweet, with her purple hair and her lace-collared dresses, but do you know what she said to me? She told me right to my face that I wasn't cut out to be a mother."

Jake knew breeding stock. With those hips, the lady was cut out, all right, although doing the job with a turkey baster was a crime against nature, if you asked him.

Which nobody had, he admitted wryly, giving his jeans another twitch.

"Priss, you must have misunderstood her. Miss Agnes means well, she just—"

"I did not! My ears are working just fine. Her exact words were that I'd do better to order me one of those great big fancy dolls from that fancy toy store because then, when I got tired of it, I could just give it away. Have you *ever*?"

Faith glanced his way again, and Jake, his face reddening under a perennial weathered tan, pretended an intense interest in a handkerchief-size quilt covered in calico butterflies. He couldn't have left now if the store was on fire.

Barely missing a beat, the two women picked up where they'd left off. "Oh, Priss, you know Miss Agnes. Her bark's a lot worse than her bite."

"It is not, either. Anyhow, I told her right flat-out that it was my money and my decision, and what's more, it's my birthday, and if I decide to have myself a baby, no busybody, who only works at the sperm bank so she'll hav a basketful of gossip to spread all over town, is going to keep me from it.''

"Priss, you didn't!''

"Well, I didn't actually tell her that last part, but I wanted to.''

"I have to admit, Miss Agnes is right about one thing,'' said Faith softly. "Having a child without a husband is no laughing matter. I should know.''

Suddenly some of the fun seemed to go out of the chase. Jake had a few memories of his own along those lines. The day he'd heard about that damned sperm bank, he'd decided that Tex Baker, the rich son-of-a-bitch who'd founded it, had to be the world's biggest hypocrite.

"Oh, I know that,'' said Priss, and the accent that had irritated Jake before didn't seem quite so irritating. "Look, I know you probably didn't go to the sperm bank, Faith— at least, that's what everybody's saying.''

Faith made a strangled sound in her throat. Honey, you've got all the tact of a cactus, Jake thought, amused, while Priss blundered on. "But if you ever want to tell somebody who the father is, you know I won't tell a soul, because I never gossip.'' Jake rolled his eyes. "And if you need some help in the shop when your time comes, you know you can count on me.''

"Thanks. I'll remember that. Beth'll be in school then, so I probably could use some help.''

Guilt was eating on him. He hadn't come in here to eavesdrop on a private conversation. A simple pick-up, that was all he'd had in mind. He ought to get the hell out of here, only his boots didn't seem to want to move in the _____ f the door.

_____ rissy—don't take this the wrong way—but Miss _____ ight. Taking a course in landscaping is one thing—I think you're real smart to do it—but having a baby is something else again.''

"Oh, for mercy's sake, Faith, I thought you, at least, would understand."

"Priss, I do understand, but—"

"No, you don't! You're just like everybody else in this stinky old town! You think I can't do anything! You think just because Daddy owned—"

Breaking off, she stood, and Jake got his first close-up, head-on look at her face. It was gorgeous. It was also red. Even as he watched, a freshet of tears spilled over her thick, dark lashes, leaving a faint trail of navy blue down her soft, freckled cheek.

Jake wanted in the worst kind of way to offer her the comfort of his arms, his lips, and any other body part she might possibly make use of. He was heartily ashamed of having listened in on a private conversation just so he could find a way to get into a woman's jeans. That was a new low, even for him. But then, he'd never pretended to be a gentleman.

In Jake's haste to get out of the Baby Boutique without embarrassing either himself or the two women, one of his big, booted feet shot out in the aisle just as the haystack blonde rushed past, and she tripped over it.

With a little deft footwork, he caught her before she could fall, but in the process, his hat was knocked to the back of his head, his knees bumped against hers, and he couldn't help himself. Right there beside a herd of woolly white polar bears, Jake squashed her up against him, belt buckle to belt buckle, and looked smack-dab into the biggest, shimmeriest pair of whiskey-brown eyes he'd ever seen on any woman.

"I do beg your pardon, ma'am...Miss Priss," he said, feeling like he'd been caught peeping in a window. Inha

ing a powdery scent that smelled like ripening corn only sweeter, he involuntarily tightened his arms, pressing every soft curve as close as he dared considering they were in a public place in broad daylight.

Faith came rushing up, all breathless and flustered. "Priss, are you all right?"

"Hmm?"

"This is—I mean, have you two met? Priss? Jake?"

A slow grin kindled in Jake's gray eyes. "I reck'n you might say we've run into each other a time or two."

Miss Pricilla Jones, who lived out on Willow Creek and was studying to be a landscaper, was blinking real hard when Jake turned his attention back to her. He promptly lost his train of thought, if he'd ever had one, as he watched her mascara melt and trickle down her velvety cheek.

"I got mascara on your hat brim," she said in a breathless little burst of apology. "I'm sorry. I hope it's not an expensive one. I'll buy you a new one if you'll tell me what size you wear. Or maybe I could just give you the money?"

It was Jake's favorite hat. He'd bought it after his first big commission, paying a hundred and fifty bucks for it. It had taken him all these years to get it broken in. "What, this old wreck?" he heard himself scoffing. "Heck, I only wear it to muck out the stalls."

She drew in a deep, shuddering breath and Jake stepped back, reluctantly putting enough space between them so that she wouldn't realize how she was affecting him. It was downright embarrassing for a man his age not to have any more control over his body.

While her friend looked on, her expression one of con-
l with just a tad of speculation, Priss blinked
xcess moisture. "Yes, well…if you're sure." She
ngle-laden arm across her face, smearing her eye

makeup even more, then she reached up with two frosted-pink-tipped fingers and rubbed the stain deeper into the beaver felt that he'd been so careful all these years not to bruise. "I heard somewhere that ginger ale was good for— or maybe it was seltzer . . ."

Ginger ale? Seltzer?

The lady didn't make a whole lot of sense to Jake, but who was keeping score? With her haystack hair tumbling down around her neck, a few strands tangling in her gaudy silver and turquoise earrings, she was sort of a mess, but she was just the kind of mess he liked. He'd have offered her five thousand bucks on the spot to go home with him and let him help her celebrate her birthday, only he didn't know how to bring up the subject without letting on he'd been eavesdropping.

Trying to think of something clever to say that would impress her with what an honorable, upstanding guy he was, he followed her outside to her peach-colored Caddy convertible, tipped his ruined hat and reluctantly opened her door.

She smiled. She had the kind of smile that would derail a locomotive, even with the little smudge of frosty pink lipstick on her left incisor.

A customer approached, and Faith, who'd been hovering in the doorway of the shop, turned, took one last worried look over her shoulder, and reluctantly went inside. Jake tried to think of some way to prolong the moment, and then decided maybe it was just as well he couldn't. Priss was evidently into babies and stuff like that, whereas Jake was a man who valued his freedom more than just about anything else. And men who valued their freedom learned pretty fast to steer clear of broody women.

Regretfully, he watched as she slid her shapely rear end across the sun-baked leather seat. Wincing, she gave him another trembly little smile and wiggled her fingers at him. He noticed that she wore three rings, but none on her third finger, left hand.

And Eddie, whoever he was, had run off to marry another woman. Jake figured the jerk must've been neutered before puberty, else he'd never have let this one get away.

He watched the Caddy roar off down Main Street and thought about what he'd learned. For all the good it was ever going to do him. Her name was Pricilla Jones. She had an expensive address. She was studying to be a landscaper. She liked stuffed animals, but she didn't have kids.

And she was thinking of going to a damned sperm bank!

Leave her be, Jake told himself, knowing there wasn't a snowball's chance in hell of that. The lady was just a mite weird, but it was a classy kind of weird. He had a feeling she might be one of those high-maintenance women. He'd had himself one of those once. It had taken him years to recover. Some lessons a man learned the hard way.

And some he never learned at all.

Feeling frustrated and slightly depressed, which was a lousy combination, he headed for the parking lot behind the hardware store where he'd left his truck. A few minutes later he was headed north, certain of only three things. Number one, that women were nuts—the haystack blonde a little more so than most.

Number two, a man was plumb out of his natural element in any store that called itself a boutique.

And number three—no matter how risky it was, sooner or later the lady in the tight jeans and the pink plastic sandals was going to wind up in his bed—bangles, mascara and all.

At age thirty-five, Jake Spencer knew himself pretty well, both shortcomings and "longcomings." He had no illusions left, and damned few ideals. What he did have was a good, solid reputation as an honest horse broker, a modest spread a few miles north of New Hope, and a powerful allergy to rich, society types.

He had both a short-term goal and a long-term goal. His short-term goal concerned the haystack blonde, and he figured he'd made a pretty good beginning. They were now on speaking terms.

As for his long-term goal, that was easy. By the time he reached forty, which was how old his old man had been when Jake was sired, he was going to be richer, meaner and one hell of a lot tougher than the old bastard had ever been.

So far, he was right on schedule on all three counts.

It was the same man. Priss had seen him around town several times, but never close enough to get a real good look. He was the kind of man a woman couldn't help but notice. Lean, lanky, with shoulders wide enough to fill a door frame and a way of walking that set loose all kinds of wicked ideas. Before she'd even met him, she'd had this tingly, excited feeling whenever she happened to see him.

Of course, he was only a wrangler. Her father would roll over in his grave if he knew she was even thinking thoughts like that about any man, much less a wrangler.

But mercy, it had certainly been a learning experience. She knew now why she'd never been able to get real steamed up over Eddie Turner, even though they'd gone together for months and she had let him kiss her with his mouth open and even unbutton her blouse.

Tripping over the wrangler's feet had been the high point in an otherwise dismal birthday. At least this time, she thought with amusement, nobody could accuse her of trying to buy friends the way they had when she'd thrown that birthday barbecue in the park last year and invited the whole town. Nobody but Faith and her mother had come until Sue Ellen had brought a handful of men over from the café, which was real sweet of her, since Sue Ellen was in the food business herself.

Priss had ended up donating the cake and barbecue to the volunteer fire department, but evidently the barbecue had sat out too long in the hot July sun. Five of the firemen had gotten sick. The whole thing had been written up in the paper, with a picture of her wearing that wretched white dress she'd worn to the debutante ball in Dallas when she was eighteen.

She'd been embarrassed to show her face around town for weeks.

But even that wasn't as bad as the party her mother had given her when she was twelve. Nora Barrington had invited six girls and six boys—sons and daughters of the town's most prominent citizens. Four had shown up. The two girls had huddled together the whole time and whispered, ignoring Priss, while the boys had tossed food and paper hats into the swimming pool and made nasty remarks about her bosoms, which had just started to grow.

But the crowning blow had come when she'd overheard Rosalie, their housekeeper, telling the cook that the beautiful Cartier watch her parents had given her for her birthday had been selected, ordered and gift-wrapped by her mother's social secretary. "Miz B., she didn't even take the time to look at the thing," the housekeeper had confided. "I'll tell you the God's honest truth, Ethel. That poor little young'un puts me in mind of them puppies folks are always dumpin' out on the side of the road, hopin' somebody'll come along and adopt 'em. Lord help the poor baby the first time some no-good man comes along and offers her a pat on the head. She'll be a-lickin' his boots from then on.''

Furious and embarrassed, Priss had flushed her new watch down the toilet, which had ruined the watch and stopped up the plumbing. As punishment, she'd been left behind when her parents went to Europe three days later.

Not that they had ever taken her on any of their other trips, but this time they had promised.

Well, she was twenty-nine years old now, not twelve. She still had Rosalie, even if both her parents were gone. As she'd never really known them, she'd never really been able to mourn them. She was old enough now to stop wishing for the moon. She was who she was, and if people didn't like her, that was just too bad, because she certainly tried her best to be friendly to everyone she ever met.

Including the man she'd nearly mowed down in Faith's place. My mercy, Priss thought, he was really something. Even better up close than he was from a distance. And the way he had looked at her—as if she were a great big bowl of Heavenly Hash ice cream....

The sky had turned dark and threatening. Lightning flashed west of town. Priss tried to remember whether or not she'd left anything out on the balcony that rain would hurt, but she couldn't concentrate. She was too busy thinking about the way Jake Spencer had made her feel. He'd been so handsome...

Well, no, he hadn't. Not really. He was too hard, too weathered, to be truly handsome. He had smelled of horse, hay, hair tonic and sweat, and as Priss pulled over to the curb to run into the drugstore for some fingernail adhesive, she had to smile, wondering if he knew how much more appealing the smell of honest sweat was than the overpowering colognes some men wore.

She was in the drugstore almost fifteen minutes—Miss Ethel was looking for denture cleanser and Priss helped her compare prices. Finally back in the car and heading south on Oak Street, she switched on the radio, which was set to her favorite country music station. Clint Black was singing about his last broken heart and it occurred to her that the cowboy in the Baby Boutique sort of looked like an older, taller, tougher version of Clint Black. He had the same kind of crinkly-eyed smile.

She wondered if the cowboy could sing. Wondered, too, if he'd felt the same jolt of static electricity she had felt when he caught her. Mercy, it had been powerful, but it was probably due to the storm.

Still, she wouldn't mind getting to know him better. Not that there was much chance of that. He looked like a wrangler, and wranglers usually hung out at Sue Ellen's Diner or Little Joe's Café, which was actually more of a saloon. Sue Ellen had better food, except for the chili, but Joe had a pool table in the back room.

Priss ate at Antonio's, when she ate out at all, which meant she probably wouldn't run into the wrangler again, because wranglers didn't patronize Antonio's.

Before heading home, Priss stopped by the hospital to drop off the toys she'd purchased at Faith's boutique, in case any of the children were asleep when she came back after supper to read bedtime stories. Toys *and* stories would probably be too much all at once. She had learned a lot about children in the year and a half she'd been volunteering in the children's ward.

Next, she went by the supermarket to pick up some frozen dinners she could microwave while Rosalie was away visiting her sister.

Finally turning off onto Willow Creek Road, she sniffed the air and decided someone must be burning stumps.

Probably taking advantage of the rain that was about to come pouring down, if the sky was anything to go by. The lightning and thunder was almost constant now. Wouldn't you just know? Priss thought. It was the crowning touch for a birthday that had gone wrong from the moment she had lost a fingernail trying to get a new tube of toothpaste out of the box.

Feeling a little bit sad, a little bit let down, Priss told herself that her birthday wasn't over yet. She still had this evening and the children. Maybe next year she'd be reading stories to her own baby.

Seeing a fire engine coming toward her, she pulled over, even though the siren wasn't sounding. Stump burning. She'd been right, then. Probably got out of bounds and started a grass fire.

Jake was halfway home, his mind partly on the upcoming sale in Dallas, partly on the haystack blonde, when a dispatcher's voice on the scanner snagged his attention.

"Fire out at Willow Creek Arms is under control."

Willow Creek?

"New Hope, head on over to a house fire at the corner of Matlock and Guntrum. Billy, stay there with the pumper truck to wet down any hot spots. South Fork's sending—"

There was a burst of static and a few more remarks, but Jake had stopped listening. Pulling a U-turn in the middle of a two-lane highway, he downshifted and roared back toward town without giving a second thought to Petemoss and the rest of the crew, who were waiting for the concrete, re-bar and forming plywood in the back of the truck to get started on the foundation of the barn extension.

Two

Priss was going a few rounds with a fireman when Jake arrived on the scene. Hair in ruins, her hands black with soot, she was gesturing wildly while the tired-looking volunteer fireman shook his head. "Ma'am, I sure wish I could, but I just cain't."

Thunder rolled overhead. The air had an eerie greenish look. "But it's safe," she argued. "You said yourself the roof wasn't going to fall in. Most of the damage to my apartment is smoke and water."

"Ma'am, rules is rules, and I've already done bent 'em right bad."

Jake noticed she was holding on to what looked like a small wooden chest, a leather case and several plastic bags bulging with various lumpy articles. "Where do you expect me to sleep? On the sidewalk?"

"I reck'n if I was you, I'd start callin' round to family.

That, or get me a room at the hotel before they're all booked up. Most folks are already gone."

"But I just got home! How was I to know—" It was then that she noticed Jake. "What are you doing here, did you get smoked out, too?"

Jake shook his head, surveying the ruin all around him. Structurally, it didn't look too bad, but it was going to take considerable cleaning before it was fit to live in.

Even so, it was pretty swank. Definitely a cut or two above Shacktown. "Heard the fire call, came to see if I could help out."

"Miz Barrington," the young fireman said earnestly, "I just cain't let you go back inside again. Goin' in for valuables, medicine and important papers—that's one thing, but I cain't let you haul out everything—if I was to let you do it, everybody else would be wanting to do it, too. Chief Clancy would be all over me like flies on a roadkill."

Barrington? As in old man Horace T. Barrington, king of the bigtime swindlers? Holy hell!

"Ma'am, maybe you'd better start callin' around for somewheres to stay tonight, else you might have to drive near 'bout to Dallas. Like I said, most folks have already gone, and there ain't that many places to stay around New Hope."

Priss swallowed hard. She was beginning to feel sick in her stomach, as if her body had been violated instead of her home. "Um, what about the bathroom? Couldn't I just go inside long enough to use the bathroom?"

"I reckon you could use the one out there by the pool. Fire didn't reach that far."

With a doleful glance over her shoulder at what used to be her home, Priss picked her way through puddles of filthy water, coiled firehoses and a few pieces of splintered furniture someone had tossed off a balcony.

Evidently she wasn't the only one who had sought refuge in the pool's dressing room. The once-white plumbing was smeared with sooty handprints, and there wasn't a clean towel to be found anywhere.

Nevertheless, several minutes later, after splashing her face and throat, she felt marginally better. At least she wasn't shaking quite so hard. Taking a deep breath, she faced herself in the mirror and groaned. Her lipstick was gone. Whatever blush remained was buried under layers of soot and streaked mascara. She looked like a speckled raccoon after a three-day binge, and as for her hair...

She groaned again. Priss had never been vain. Her mother had seen to that, constantly harping on the fact that she must take after her father's side of the family, because no one on *her* side had ever had freckles and such common, peasant-type bone structure.

Nora Barrington, tall, reed-slender, with black hair and skin the color of a magnolia petal, had come from one of those Virginia families that was reputed to be older than God.

Priss had been a disappointment to her father because she wasn't a son, and to her mother because she wasn't a beauty. After she'd graduated from Mary Washington, in a deliberate attempt to prove she didn't care, she had patterned herself after the most outrageously feminine country singer she could think of.

It had driven them both wild.

Jake was waiting outside the pool house door when she emerged, her face scrubbed right down to the freckles and her own straw-colored lashes. She felt as if someone had carved out a great big hollow place in her stomach, and it was going to take more than a fresh layer of makeup to fix it.

Priss tried and almost succeeded in ignoring the man. What she wanted to do was to run and hide, only there was no place to hide. She could barricade herself inside the bathroom again, but that wouldn't solve anything. The best she could do was summon up the attitude her mother used to call presence.

She tried. It was simply too much trouble. Besides, as much as she would like to find a scapegoat to pin all her troubles on, Jake Spencer wasn't it.

Her shoulders slumped. Jake stepped forward. She stepped back. If he touched her right now, she was going to come apart, and she knew as well as she knew her own name that once she did, not all the king's horses nor all the king's men would be able to put her together again.

Which reminded her of something else. She'd have to call the hospital to see if one of the other volunteers could read to the children—she'd never be able to make it now.

"Well? What are you hanging around for?" she snapped. "Aren't you through gawking?"

He was just standing there, in his worn jeans, his sweat-stained work shirt and his pearl-gray Stetson with the mascara-stained brim, looking calm and tough and arrogant all at the same time. It was more than any woman could take under the circumstances. "Don't you have anything better to do?"

Gratuitous rudeness had never been her style, but at this point, Priss was beyond caring.

"Honey, are you sure you're all right?"

Her chin quivered. She tightened her grubby fists and tried to hang on to her attitude. "No, dammit, I am not all right! My apartment is ruined, and I'm late for an appointment, and... and I forgot to get my hair-dryer!"

Jake eyed the jumble of parcels she'd parked on the poolside chaise longue. "What's all that stuff?"

"What it is, is none of your business," she retorted.

What it was, was her mother's second-best set of flat-ware—the best set, a complete service for twenty-four, had been sold at the auction three years ago. With the fireman hovering over her every step of the way, she had only had time to dump her makeup drawer into a plastic bag, snatch up her hair rollers and a change of underwear, and grab her new Clint Black CD. She'd clean forgotten about her jewelry case and her hair-dryer.

"Oh, for pity's sake, it's just some odds and ends I needed," she muttered. "I asked you what you were do-ing here."

"Like I said," he explained patiently, "I heard the call on the fire channel and thought you could use a hand."

Priss could have used more than a hand, she could have used a place to stay. She could have used her walk-in closet full of clothes, and she definitely could have used her best friend and housekeeper, Rosalie, who had practically raised her.

What was Rosalie going to think when she got back and the apartment was such a mess? Oh, my mercy, she would have to call and warn her.

Drawing in a deep breath, she willed herself to remain calm, but it wasn't easy. One look at those steady, silver-gray eyes and it was all she could do not to throw herself into Jake's arms and cry her eyes out. Which didn't make sense, because in the first place, she didn't even know the man, and in the second place, she never cried.

Well...hardly at all. Naturally she'd cried when her mother had died, but except for that she hadn't shed a tear since she was eight years old and had fallen out of a tree and broken her arm. She'd been showing off for the gar-dener's son, who'd been ten at the time but who couldn't climb a step stool.

Actually, there had been one other time when she'd cried, the year she'd gone off to college. Priss had been barely seventeen when she'd overheard Mike Russo telling a visiting cousin that messing around with Prissy Barrington wasn't worth the risk, because her old man had put out the word that any guy who did would wind up singing in the soprano section of the choir.

Embarrassed to tears and mad as a hornet, she had drunk up half a bottle of her father's most expensive French wine and cried until she got sick and threw up, but that was absolutely the last time she'd ever shed a tear.

"Look, I really appreciate your concern," she said, once more in control of her voice. "I'm just fine, thanks. I don't need anybody." There were things she had to do, but first she had to get herself organized, and she could hardly do that under the glare of those steely gray eyes.

The young fireman came back, sloshing through puddles of dirty water on the turquoise pool surround. "Ma'am, I'm leaving now, but I just wanted you to know, the place'll be guarded. You don't have to worry none about looting or anything like that. Soon as things cool down some, they'll start the inspection. In a few days we'll know how long it'll be before you can move back in."

"A few days," she wailed.

"I've got a phone in my truck," Jake said. "Why don't we start calling around? If the hotel's full, we can try that new motel out near the airport."

Up went the chin again. A motel? Barringtons didn't stay in motels. "Thanks, but I'll be staying with friends." Priss shied away from the fact that the only friend she would even consider asking for help was Faith Harper, and she happened to know that Faith's place would never fit the two of them.

"Fine, then we'll call your friend and tell her you're on your way. Honey, you don't want to hang around here any longer. There's a fresh batch of thunderheads making up over to the west."

Priss glanced over her shoulder. Oh, fine. Just what she needed. More water on her leaky apartment.

"Besides, you're starting to shake again. You look like hell, and—"

"Really, I can't tell you how much better that makes me feel." She glared at him, but her heart wasn't in it. "Oh, all right. If you insist, I'll let you help me carry this stuff out to my car."

"Thanks," Jake said, his voice deceptively soft. What he ought to do was throw the lady over his shoulder, haul her off to the nearest hotel and dump her in the lobby. Now that he could see past her butt, what he saw was the kind of female he'd always gone out of his way to avoid. Spoiled little rich girls who pranced around like they were shod in solid gold.

On the other hand, it didn't take much to see that this spoiled little rich girl was barely hanging in there. Somewhat to his surprise, Jake admitted that in a little less than a couple of hours, what had started out as a simple, wholesome case of lust had run the gamut from amusement to dislike, and was rapidly turning into a grudging case of admiration.

Gathering up an armload of boxes and bags, he followed her down the shallow steps to the parking lot, which was almost empty except for a utility truck and a pumper. The fireman was right. She was getting a late start on finding herself another bunk.

Over in the far corner behind the utility truck, Jake spotted the peach-colored tail fin just before he saw her stop short and heard what sounded almost like a moan, but might have been thunder. Setting his load down on a raised flower bed, he hurried forward just as Priss dropped out of view. By the time he reached her, she was on her knees, stroking a crumpled fender that was wrapped halfway around her left rear tire. Someone had evidently been in one hell of a hurry to get out of there.

"I don't believe it," Priss wailed. "I just don't believe it! Do you know, this has been absolutely the worst birthday of my entire life?"

Jake could commiserate. From what he'd seen so far, it sure hadn't been cupcakes and lemonade. Stroking his chin and trying to look judicious, he walked around her car, surveying it from all angles. He had a feeling even touching up a scratch on one of these vintage babies was no small deal, but then, what did he know? His auto repair skills began and ended with baling wire and duct tape.

"Frame might not be bent, but I doubt if you can drive it like that, even if I could pry out the fender."

"I don't know who to call first, the hotel or the body shop."

"I thought you were going to stay with friends."

"Oh, don't bother me with details now!"

"Right. Okay, honey, if you want to hang around here and figure it out, I reckon I might as well shove off." He took a long look at the towering thunderheads, another at the row of damaged apartments, and then made as if to leave.

No way was he going to leave her there, but Jake knew a thing or two about dealing with women.

"Wait—that is, if you don't mind staying another few minutes, could you please just wait here until I find out where I'm going to be staying?"

There—that wasn't so hard, was it? She'd even said please. "No problem," Jake replied easily. Standing at ease, he figured he could give her about five minutes before those clouds busted right wide open.

The young fireman slogged over to the utility truck, his boots making almost as much noise as the rumbling thunder. "Ma'am, you don't want to be hanging around here with that storm coming up. I heard tell you're expectin', and I know for a fact that it don't take much to upset a woman when she's in the fam—"

Priss stood slowly. "You heard *what?*"

Glancing from Priss to Jake and back again, he said, "I think it was Miss Ethel that said—I ran into her at the post office this morning when I went by to mail-order me some—that is, she said you were by that baby place out on the highway this morning, and—"

Priss said a word Jake didn't think ladies even knew, her face about three shades pinker than her car. Shifting his position, he moved in beside her and slung an arm casually over her shoulder. Like she'd been doing it all her life, she leaned into his side.

Jake cleared his throat. "Son, you don't want to put too much stock in town talk. Some folks got nothing better to do than flap tongues."

Priss nudged closer to her newfound protector. "Miss Ethel never told a true story in all her life," she declared, and the fireman nodded nervously. Sweating under his heavy gear, he backed toward the utility truck.

Jake figured it was time to change the subject. "Maybe we'd better get on with those phone calls, Priss."

The lady was not to be distracted. "I know how it happened. Miss Agnes told Miss Minny about—well, about something I was thinking about doing, and Miss Minny must have told Miss Ethel, and by the time Miss Ethel found somebody to pass on the story to, she'd got it all mixed up, as usual."

The fireman's gaze dropped to her flat stomach just before he swung up into the driver's seat, and Jake decided things had gone far enough. "Come on now, honey, before that lightning gets any closer. I hope you stuck in a decent pair of shoes while you were packing."

"Shoes?" She blinked, having apparently forgotten that his arm was still around her, practically welding her to his side.

Reluctantly, Jake gave her some space. "Those, uh, things you're wearing are right pretty, but I wouldn't want you to get a charley horse trying to walk in 'em."

"My Jellies are perfectly comfortable, but thank you for your concern."

"Jellies. Uh-huh."

Priss knew he was just trying to be kind to her, and she appreciated it, she really did. Only she was having trouble hanging on to what little bit of pride she had left, and Jake's kindness was distracting. Under the circumstances, even noticing the way he made her feel when he touched her was downright unnatural.

She could hardly go to Faith's, and by now the hotel was probably full. She'd have to call a cab and head for Dallas, because there was no way she was going to sleep in some chintzy little motel with airplanes taking off right over her bed.

Jake started gathering up her parcels just as a streak of lightning split the sky wide open. "Come on, honey, you need a friend and I'm offering my services."

"I have plenty of friends, thanks." She had Faith. And Rosalie, who was in Dallas visiting her sister. And the preacher and his wife, because she had paid for an exterminator to deal with the cockroaches that had infested the parsonage. They'd been too embarrassed to talk about it until she'd found out about it accidentally.

And of course, her kids at the hospital, because she read to them a couple of times a week. And she'd come to know a few of the staff there.

Reaching for her wooden chest, she said, "That sounded real rude, didn't it? And here you came all this way out of the kindness of your heart."

Jake let it pass. It wasn't his heart he'd been thinking about when he'd set out to pick her up that afternoon, although he had to admit it might've given an extra thump or two back there when she'd been hanging on to him like trumpet vine on a fence post.

The first drops of rain drilled down like a hail of bullets just as he reached through the open window of his dusty pickup and opened the passenger door. Ever since it had been kicked in by a riled-up stallion, the latch didn't work half the time. "Come on, get in," he said, tossing her things into the jump seat. "Give me your car keys."

Without a single protest, she handed them over, then climbed into the truck while he raised the top of her convertible and locked the doors. He was wet by the time he climbed in beside her, switched on the ignition and backed out of the parking lot.

Out on the highway, he cut her a quick glance. She had a defeated look about her that worried him. In fact, this whole business was beginning to give him a spooky feeling, like trouble was about to blindside him and there wasn't a blamed thing he could do about it.

Part of it was the way she looked—part of it the way she smelled, all clean and sweet and womany. Part of it was the way she felt when she huddled up beside him, hanging on to his arm, letting him protect her.

And part of it was because she was a broody female and he was a horny male, which was a downright dangerous combination.

All things considered, Jake decided that this hadn't been one of his better ideas. The minute he discovered that every time he laid a hand on her, certain reflexes kicked in, he should've tipped his hat and walked away.

Now that it was too late, he had an idea that Miss Barrington, fancy pedigree and all, was going to be more of a handful than he'd bargained on.

Priss's social skills, never particularly high, were at an all-time low by the time they finally passed Buck's Texaco and Barbecue and headed out of town. She told herself it was only because she had never been burned out of her home before. A thing like that could knock the starch out of anybody.

But it wasn't only the fire. Part of it had to do with the man beside her. With his hat pulled down low on his forehead, he looked grim and dangerously masculine—more like Clint Eastwood than Clint Black. She couldn't believe she had let herself be talked into going home with a perfect stranger just because both the hotel and the motel were full.

And in his truck, too—not even her own car. Not that she felt much like driving, even if she could. The way her luck was running, she'd have wrapped her car around a telephone pole before she even got past the city limits.

"Is it very far?" Suddenly she was bone tired.

"Few more miles." He'd been saying that ever since they passed the last stop sign on the way out of town. "The garage has probably picked up your car by now." He'd called right after he'd checked the hotel and motel.

"Where exactly did you say it was?"

"Your car?"

"Your home."

"Oh. The Bar Nothing. It's up the road about half a dozen more miles."

"Is that what you call it?"

"Is that what I call what?"

"Your home. The Bar Nothing?" Priss knew she was chattering, she couldn't help it. She always chattered when she was nervous.

Clint Black Eastwood shot her a cool glance. "That's what it says over the main gate."

She twisted the bangles on her arm. Her mother would have called them gaudy. Her mother thought anything more colorful than basic black, worn with pearls and a touch of gold, was gaudy, which was why Priss had sort of gone overboard after her mother died. It had driven her father wild.

She stared at the big booted foot on the accelerator and wondered if Jake thought she was gaudy. She wondered if he thought she was sexy. Goodness knows she tried to be, not that it had ever done her much good. Her father had ruined her chances with the entire male population of New Hope, first with threats, then with promises.

According to her mother, who had never gotten over her Virginia-hood, the people of New Hope, Texas, "Simply aren't *our kind of people.*"

Later on, after her mother had died, her father had told her during one of their rare conversations that the only reason anyone would take up with her was because of *who she was.*

Priss had come to hate who she was.

According to Horace Taylor Barrington, that went double for any man who showed any interest in her. Money-grubbers, every last one of them. When the time came for her to marry, he would find her a husband from among *the right people.*

Her parents had had a way of speaking in italics. Or maybe she only remembered them that way.

Jake slowed down as they approached a long, potholed driveway. There were pastures on both sides, some brown, some green. Off in the distance, Priss could see several horses, an enormous barn and a circular pen.

Priss didn't know very much about pastures. She knew even less about horses, although at school back east she had let on that she did. Virginia was big on horses, and on learning that she was from Texas, everyone had taken it for granted that she'd grown up riding. One thing she'd inherited from both her parents was pride and a real disinclination to admit her shortcomings, although she was working on it. So first she'd pretended a disdain for eastern saddles, then a bad back. After a while, no one had bothered her about riding.

The arched sign over the entrance said in block letters, The Bar Nothing. "It's not very original, is it?" she observed, wanting to take him down a notch for reasons she didn't even try to understand.

"Not particularly. You got a problem with it?"

Squirming under the focus of those steady gray eyes, Priss felt guilty at her meanness. "I shouldn't have said that. It's a nice name. I guess what I meant is that the whole idea is sort of silly. Naming houses and land and all. I mean, it's really kind of pretentious, don't you think?"

"Reckon I'm just a pretentious sort of guy."

Priss winced as gravel bounced up and struck the underside of the fenders, sounding like a barrage of hail. He drove too fast, but then, so did she. "I don't think you are," she said earnestly. Unclipping her seat belt, she turned toward him, tucking her knee up on the bench seat. "Pretentious, that is. In fact, I think you're really pretty ordinary." That didn't sound right, either. "What I mean is, you don't look as if you care how you look—I mean—"

The glance he sent her was almost pitying. "Why don't you just kick back and relax, sugar? Once we get there you'll want to check the place out, get settled in, maybe make a few more phone calls to let folks know where you're staying."

"By now, Miss Agnes probably has me visiting the White House."

Jake chuckled. Priss sighed, stared through the bug-spattered windshield, and wondered who she could call.

Faith, probably. Faith had introduced them, after all—mercy, had it only been a few hours ago?

Faith was the only one who understood why Priss shopped in Dallas instead of New Hope. Priss had always shopped in Dallas simply because that's where her mother had taken her to shop. After her mother had died, Priss had overheard someone saying that the Barringtons had always thought they were too good to spend their money in a little town like New Hope, so naturally, after that she'd been too self-conscious to shop at home except for Faith's place and a few incidentals.

As they pulled up beside an unpainted frame house set among a scattering of outbuildings, all of which were in far better condition than the house itself, she wondered what her parents would say if they could see her now, riding in a battered pickup that sported duct tape on the seats and a dented door, being driven by a common wrangler who wore sweaty work clothes and dusty, worn-out boots.

They'd say he was not *her kind of people*.

And they'd be absolutely right. Jake Spencer wasn't anybody's kind of people, he was one of a kind. A kind that was totally alien to a woman who was still too embarrassed to buy *Cosmopolitan* off a newsstand, who until recently had thought the Kama Sutra was a book of poetry, and who had yet to see her first adult movie.

"Welcome to the Bar Nothing," he drawled, making it sound like a salacious threat.

Or maybe a promise.

Then he grinned, and Priss told herself she was just being silly. The fire, coming right on top of her disastrous visit to the sperm bank that morning, had simply thrown her imagination into overdrive.

She tried to think of something nice to say about his ugly house, but there wasn't a whole lot to be said. There weren't even any flowers or shrubs to soften the stark outlines. "It, um, it looks solid."

"Ye-ep." He dropped the keys in his shirt pocket, probably, she thought, embarrassed, because there was no room in his blue jeans. Without even looking, she knew precisely where they were frayed the most. The knees, the seat and the—

It was all she could do to keep her gaze away from his lap.

Oh, for mercy's sake, Pricilla Joan, grow up!

"What I mean is, it looks okay, but some shrubbery and flower beds would be nice. The shutters could stand a coat of paint, too, but then, I suppose they're more for protection against the weather than for show."

When he didn't reply, she slid him a sidelong glance. Were his lips twitching at the corners, or was that her imagination? She tried to think of anything she had said that could possibly be construed as funny.

Jake reached across her and opened her door, causing her to suck in her breath sharply. "Come on inside and we'll get you settled. I need to ride out for a couple of hours. How're you feeling, still pretty wobbly?"

She was so pale every freckle on her face stood out like cayenne pepper on a fried egg. "Not at all wobbly," she said, and he gave her full marks for grit. Walking across the barren yard under a stingy spattering of rain, he attempted to pull her against his side again, telling himself it was because she looked like she could use the support.

She stopped him cold. "I don't like being touched."

Jake's eyebrows shot skyward. "Is that a fact?" he drawled, thinking back to all the times in the past few hours when she'd burrowed against his side like a mouse trying to get into a corncrib.

She took off toward the front steps, and Jake hung back to admire the action. Those damned crazy shoes of hers ought to be against the law, but he'd fight the man who tried to outlaw 'em.

She was probably right, though. No more touching. He just might be able to stand it long enough for her to get her place squared away.

He'd damned well better stand it, if he knew what was good for him. Every time he laid a finger on her he felt like a beer that had been rolling around in the back of the truck under a hot sun and then opened too fast.

Fizzy.

If there was one thing Jake Spencer was sure of—at least when his glands weren't doing his thinking for him—it was that he was too old to feel fizzy about any woman.

Another thing he was pretty sure of was that Baker's bastard had no business fooling around with Barrington's brat.

Three

Thunder started low in the southeast, rumbled overhead and then faded off to the northeast before dying out. By then another barrage had commenced. It was no longer raining hard, but Priss ran to keep her hair from getting wet, which sent more of it tumbling down around her shoulders. She could hear Jake's feet pounding the hard-packed ground right behind her.

The air smelled of wet dust. Standing on the front porch, she shook the drops off her assorted plastic bags while she glanced around at a wide swing that dangled from a broken rusted chain, a dead tomato plant in a plastic container, and a set of window shades that hung crookedly inside the front windows, jealously guarding the rooms from the blistering July heat. At least the showers had cooled things down. That was one blessing she could count in what had turned out to be a dismal day.

Jake reached around her to open the front door. It was one of those metal storm doors—newer, but no prettier than the rest of the place. It truly was an ugly house, she thought, wondering how it would look with a coat of paint—maybe yellow—with dark green shutters and some oleanders, and maybe a few hibiscus, and lots of orange and yellow annuals, with soft, gray Russian Olives to set it off....

Her mother had insisted on having boxwoods and tea roses, although the boxwoods had never done well. The gardener had given Priss her own little garden when she was six, where she'd scattered dozens of packs of seeds, mixing daisies and onions, petunias and nasturtiums and turnips. She had loved it.

"Mercy, it's freezing in here!" Priss stood in the center of the hall, shivering in the frigid interior air, and peered through the open door to the left and the doorless opening to the right. As far as she could see, the walls were all the same dingy shade of white. The floors had once been painted battleship gray, but the paint had long since worn off, showing traffic patterns down the hall, into the kitchen and, to a lesser degree, back to the bottom of the stairs. Nobody seemed to use the living room, and after one quick glance inside, Priss could see why. She had seen flea markets with more style.

In the kitchen to the left, she could see a wooden table, also painted gray—but with the paint scrubbed off the top—three chairs and a shiny, new side-by-side refrigerator that made the whole room look even shabbier. The only decoration, as far as she could see, was a thermometer advertising a local heating and air-conditioning company and a feed store calendar tacked high on the wall and hanging crooked.

Standing behind her and slightly to one side, Jake studied his home through the eyes of a stranger. It had been a long time since he'd even looked at it at all. As a place to eat, to sleep, and to work, it was sufficient. He had an office off the kitchen where his computer and his books were kept, along with a recliner and a magazine rack overflowing with back issues of *Western Horseman, Farm and Ranch Trader,* and half a week's worth of newspapers he'd not yet gotten around to reading.

He hadn't seen the inside of her place on Willow Creek Road, but even messed up with smoke and water, it was bound to be a whole lot better than his. The thought made him feel defensive, and as Jake had never much cared for feeling defensive, he got mad instead.

"Dump your gear in the the guest room. Upstairs, last door on the left. Bath's across the hall. Make yourself at home. I'm going out for a spell." He tossed the words in jerky little bunches over his shoulder on his way to the front door, which he couldn't slam even if he wanted to, on account of the compressed air gadget that took its own sweet time, no matter how damned mad he was.

"Well, mercy me, aren't you a sweet one," Priss murmured, amused, surprised, but not hurt. After all, she hadn't pushed herself off on him, he'd been the one to insist. She'd just as soon have gone to the hotel. They could have found a place for her somewhere if she'd insisted. If there was one thing she had learned from her daddy it was that no door was ever really closed if H. T. Barrington wanted it open, only she'd never been good at pushing her way in where she wasn't wanted.

Taking Jake at his word, Priss climbed the stairs in search of the guest room, hoping it was better than what she'd seen so far.

It wasn't. There was an iron bed, a plastic veneer night-stand, an old-fashioned chiffonier with drawers that stuck, and a chair that matched those in the kitchen except for the rung that had been broken and patched with duct tape. The bed frame was painted gray, obviously with paint left over from the floors and the kitchen table. It was stark naked, the mattress covered in yellowed blue-and-white ticking. She decided then and there to turn the mattress before she made the bed.

It occurred to her that the ticking was the same blue-and-white striped material that had looked just fine in the raincoat she'd bought from Neiman Marcus some years ago, only her raincoat had been trimmed with a red collar and cuffs and fancy brass buttons, whereas the mattress sported only a rust-brown stain and a few gray cotton tufts.

A slash of hard rain struck the side of the house, ham-mering on the tall, uncurtained windows. Priss told her-self she was lucky to have a roof over her head at all. If it hadn't been for Jake, she would probably still be standing out by the swimming pool arguing with that poor fire-man. She purely hated to lose an argument when she knew she was in the right.

Well. Whining wasn't going to get anything accom-plished.

First she located a broom and commenced to sweeping, which raised more dust than it removed, but at least it made her feel better. Action always did, but along with her kitchen, Rosalie guarded her mops, brooms and vacuum cleaner like a dragon. So when Priss was feeling upset, she usually made do with playing a few games of tennis when she could find someone to play with her, or swimming a few lengths of the pool when she couldn't, or messing about in the flower beds—which upset the super whenever he caught her at it, but she did it anyway.

When none of that worked and she was feeling really needy, she went for a long, fast drive in the country with the top down.

The linen closet Priss finally located was in no better condition than the rest of the house. It smelled of pine oil and mothballs instead of her favorite gardenia sachets, but at least the sheets were clean. She looked for a pretty spread, but the best she could find was a cotton plaid that, after years of hard water and harsh sun, had faded to shades of gray, olive drab and khaki.

She dusted off the furniture with her lace-edged, monogrammed handkerchief, wrinkled her nose at the results, then looked automatically for the pink satin laundry bag that hung on the back of her closet door at home, where she always put things she could rinse out with toilet soap. Rosalie allowed her to do her own hand wash, but like the rest of her cleaning equipment, Rosalie's washer and dryer were off limits. Priss had never really had any burning desire to wash clothes or clean house, but it was the frustration of not being allowed to do it that irritated her.

Peering out into the hallway to make sure she was still alone in the house, she set out to explore. She found the bath, which was just about what she expected. Antique plumbing, the gloss long since worn off the old cast-iron tub, and a speckled mirror. There were two more bedrooms, with male clothing draped over chairs, bedsteads, dressers, and a few more articles scattered on the floor alongside several pairs of boots.

Downstairs, she found a pantry with rows of canned goods, mostly tomatoes, chili beans and peaches, a set of wooden bins that weren't labeled, an upright vacuum cleaner that had been webbed in by an industrious spider, a bucket and a mop.

Feeling like a trespasser, she opened another door off the kitchen and found what was obviously an office of some sort. It was no prettier than the rest of the house and not even as neat. There were several framed horse pictures on the wall, and a photograph of a group of men standing beside a racetrack that looked more eastern than western. The men all wore suits and Panama hats; only one wore a Stetson.

She wanted to take a closer look, to see if Jake was the one in the Stetson, but she was too embarrassed. He had invited her to make herself at home, but that didn't mean she could pry into his personal belongings.

Last of all she found what must be a utility room. There was a chest-type freezer, what she supposed was a hot water heater, and something that might be a heat pump—then again, it might not. Priss was no expert on the machinery that kept a house operating smoothly. Her father's staff had included two maintenance engineers who saw to that sort of thing.

In the corner, under a shelf that held what looked like a fifty-pound box of detergent and half hidden under still more dirty clothes, was a machine she recognized as a washing machine. Beside it was a gleaming white dryer so new it still had the stickers attached.

Which was a good thing, because it was raining up a storm outside and except for underwear, she hadn't thought to bring along a change of clothes, not even so much as a nightgown. She'd been so certain she'd be able to go back inside once all the hubbub died down.

Now everything she was wearing was damp and stained with soot, and if there was one thing Priss couldn't stand, it was to be dirty.

While she was at it, she might as well gather up what needed washing from the other two bedrooms. She might not have inherited much from her parents, but she had definitely inherited an overdose of pride from somewhere. One other thing she could never stand, along with being dirty, was being beholden.

It was several hours later when Jake drove into the yard. He'd been down at the training pen, working a roan stud that was about as ornery as a three-legged jackass, especially with the weather spitting rain and lightning the way it was. They'd gone a round or two just that morning, with Jake coming up on the short end. This time, they'd called it a draw.

God, he was tired. And filthy. And wet.

He peeled off his shirt and slung it over onto the passenger seat. He was almost too tired to make it upstairs to the bathroom. What he should've done was sluice down at the horse trough, but he'd been in a hurry to get home.

So much for working Priss out of his system.

While he was rubbing the roan down, Petemoss had come into the barn and Jake had asked him if he'd mind bunking down in the tack room for a night or so.

"Got ye a womun up there, ain't che?" The arthritic old ex-rodeo clown had slapped his good knee and spit a stream of tobacco.

"It's not what you think," Jake had protested.

"Heck, I can't even remember what it is I do think when it comes to wimmen!"

"Yeah, well . . . her place was smoked up real bad in a fire. She's sort of a friend of a friend, you might say. I felt obliged to offer her a place to stay until she can get straight."

"Why? Can't the friend put 'er up?"

"I didn't ask."

"You the one set 'er house on fire?"

"No, dammit. Lightning hit it. And it's not a house, it's an apartment. And anyhow, it wasn't hers that burned. They all got messed up, though, and she can't stay there until the inspectors go through the place and it gets put back together again. Now, are you going to cut me some slack, or aren't you?"

"Sure, sonny, I'll cut ye all the slack ye need to hang yerse'f, on'y don't come crying to me when she's got ye thrown, tied and branded. Who's gonna cook fer ye? She gonna make ye breakfast in bed?"

"No, dammit, and it's not like that! I can cook. Hell, we can eat out of cans. It won't be for more than a day or two, anyhow. I just thought she might feel uncomfortable in a house with two strange men."

"I ain't strange. Got me a few doubts about you, boy. But me, I'm just as natur'l as the flowers in May."

Jake made a rude noise, and Pete made a few more cracks, which Jake pretty much ignored. The old man didn't have much to laugh about, being so busted up after a lifetime of rodeoing that about all he could do was cook and keep house.

They were a pair, all right, Jake thought as he rattled up a pockmarked dirt road that turned slick as boiled okra every time it rained. It had been restlessness that had driven him away, but he was beginning to feel guilty about going off and leaving Priss alone in an empty house. He'd thought to work some of the tetchiness out of his system so he could take things nice and easy, keep a cool head on his shoulders.

All it took to set him off again was seeing the clothesline full of laundry sagging in the driving rain. What the devil was she up to now? Dammit, those were *his* jeans hanging there, getting spattered with mud. And wasn't that—hell, yes! It was his favorite shirt, hanging by the collar, getting stretched all out of shape.

He floored the accelerator, feeling the tires slide as they shot across rainslick ruts. It served him right, letting his hormones lead him into a damn fool situation like this. He could have found her a place to stay without inviting her to move in with him. There were still a few women in town who wouldn't mind doing him a favor.

What the devil had he hoped to achieve?

Well, he knew what he had hoped to achieve, all right. What he hadn't counted on was coming down with a bad case of honor at the last minute. Jake had never claimed to be a gentleman—his tongue wouldn't wrap around a lie that big—but neither was he scoundrel enough to take advantage of a woman who was a guest under his own roof, not when she'd been practically forced into the position of accepting his hospitality by a streak of personal misfortune.

As he jogged across the front yard, lightning ripped the sky apart, illuminating the clothesline Petemoss had strung up until they could get the new dryer wired in.

Jake did a double take. That couldn't be his—

Oh, hell, it was. His brand new black silk shirt, also hanging by the collar, and a pair of light-tan, worsted, western-cut pants that were part of a suit he'd had tailor-made in Dallas. They looked about five sizes too small now.

So much for his wheeling-and-dealing outfit. He'd left them out on a chair, meaning to drop them off at the cleaner's next time he went to town, only he kept forgetting because, hell—it wasn't like he wore them every other day.

Now she'd ruined them. Just like she'd ruined his best hat.

Jake was mad as hot pitch all over again—madder than a suit of clothes could account for. He could afford to buy himself a dozen suits and silk shirts, and anyhow, the only time he ever wore anything other than work clothes was when he went to a sale in Kentucky.

Kentucky folks were different. They had what you might call a dress code. Here in Texas or in Oklahoma, everybody dressed pretty much the same at a working sale. The only way to tell the wranglers from the owners from the brokers was to wait to see who got sent out for coffee.

It sure as hell wouldn't be the owners or the brokers.

But dammit, that woman had no call to go invading his privacy, jangling her jewelry in his bedroom where he had to sleep every night—smelling up the place with her perfume!

Jake's anger was all mixed up with the sexual energy that had been seething inside him ever since he'd first caught sight of Priss tooling down Main Street earlier that day. He leapt onto the front porch. His wet boot soles, slick as creek mud on the painted surface, skidded so that he had to grab hold of the storm door handle to steady himself, which riled him even more.

"Woman, what the devil do you think you're doing?" he roared before he was even inside the house. He stomped down the hall, loaded for bear, just as she appeared in the kitchen doorway.

He'd clean forgot about leaving his shirt in the truck, but when he saw where she was staring—saw how her eyes got big as a pair of billiard balls, he felt like hiding behind the door and begging her pardon.

"Jake?" She sounded breathless.

He wondered if it was because of his scars, or because of something else. His gaze dropped to the front of her shirt, and he pictured her in the same condition he was in. Although, come to think of it, it was physically impossible for a woman to be in the same condition he was in at the moment. What he needed wasn't a shirt, it was one of Pete's damned ruffled aprons.

"I, um, I wasn't sure what time you wanted supper, but I was hungry, so I made pancakes and sausage. I hope that's all right?"

She was squeaking like a mouse, bless her sweet buns. "Yeah, I reckon it's long gone suppertime. What with the storm and all, it kind of snuck up on me."

Her eyes were the color of sourwood honey. Of good whiskey. Of creek water running clear over a bed of rocks. She was smiling, sort of half hopeful, half fearful, like she was waiting for his approval, but not really expecting it.

"Sounds great," he said, the dregs of his anger fizzing out like air from a flat tire on an eighteen-wheeler. He hated pancakes. Hated waffles or anything that had to be sopped in syrup to make it edible. Pete was the pancake man. "I'm real partial to sausage patties."

"Patties?"

"Cakes. You know—the way you cook bulk sausage."

She looked sort of doubtful, but then she smiled again and it was like the sun coming out through a bank of dark storm clouds. Jake had a sinking feeling he was in even more trouble than he'd thought.

"I'd better clean up and put on some clothes," he said, and the doubtful look was back.

"Oh. Um, I'm not sure, but I don't think you have any more shirts. As soon as it slacks up some, I'll bring in the wash and hang it in the kitchen to finish drying, but I couldn't get the dryer to work. Oh, and I borrowed some clothes—I hope you don't mind?"

She was chattering like a squirrel. He figured she was either nervous or cold, and as she was wearing one of his flannel shirts over a pair of Pete's old long johns, she couldn't be too cold.

Actually, they looked sort of cute on her, like the tights and big tops a lot of women were wearing these days. He wondered what she'd do if he demanded his shirt back. If he backed her into a corner and started to unbutton it real slow, and then eased it off her breasts, over her shoulders, down her arms...

Oh boy. This wasn't going to work.

Jake crossed to the thermostat and nudged the temperature down another couple of degrees. "I could've told you the dryer's not hooked up yet if you'd thought to ask," he grumbled.

He headed for the stairs to wash up, and she followed along behind him, talking all the way. If she was going to follow him up to the bathroom, Jake decided, with the way he was feeling right now, they might as well skip supper and get on with dessert.

He made it halfway up the stairs before his stomach growled noisily. On the verge of begging her pardon, he bit back the words. Dammit, it was his belly and his house, and if she was offended, why then, that was just tough. Working off a bad case of the willies—not to mention a wagonload of frustration—gave a man an appetite.

So now he had two kinds of appetite to deal with.

"So that's why I couldn't get it to work," she was saying in that finishing school drawl of hers that was beginning to grow on him. "I thought it was just me. I've never been real good with...you know—stuff. Oh, and I looked in the freezer, but everything was frozen. So I just cooked what was in the refrigerator. The sausage, I mean. There was only one egg, so I made pancakes. I think you're supposed to put eggs in the flour, aren't you?''

That was when Jake started to have doubts.

"Anyway, they're all done, so you go ahead and change for dinner and I'll just go pour the wine. I'm afraid it's only screw top—I couldn't find your good wine.''

"The wine?''

She had already turned away. Now she glanced over her shoulder. With her hair stacked loose and sexy and his shirt falling halfway down her thighs, she was enough to fuel a year's worth of night sweats.

Jake cleared his throat. "The only wine I know of is Pete's private stash of arthritis medicine.''

"Oh. I'm afraid I opened it already. To breathe, you know.''

"To breathe. Right.'' He hoped the wine was having more luck breathing than he was. Priss looked even better in Pete's long johns than she did in tight jeans.

"See you in the front room as soon as you're ready, all right?''

All wrong. When the devil had he lost control of his own home?

And what was that business about the front sitting room? Nobody ever used the front sitting room. It was too grim for anything short of a wake.

She had cleared the junk off the old mission oak table, dragged it to the center of the room, covered it with a tablecloth she'd found God knew where, and set it with the flowered dishes Pete had bought at a salvage place, which nobody ever used because they were so damned ugly.

Evidently she'd ferreted out his supply of emergency candles, too. Candlelight and wine. Hell's bells. Maybe he

ought to go down to the barn and drag Pete back up here.
There was safety in numbers.

"I couldn't find a pitcher for the syrup," she said, "so
I used this."

This being a china vase that had been sitting on the
mantel over the boarded-up fireplace ever since Pete had
won it at a church bingo game. It was even uglier than the
china.

Priss was pouring the wine when he came up behind her.
Jake had never been much of a wine man. Generally he
stuck to Red Dog and Wild Turkey, but Pete claimed his
doctor swore by the grape, saying it would add years to a
man's life.

"I'm not sure what time it is—my watch is in the shop
and I couldn't find a clock, but dinner's all ready, so if you
want to sit down, I'll bring it in."

Jake didn't know what time it was, either. Unless he was
off at a sale, he didn't rely much on clocks. Sunup was
time enough to start working. Quitting time was when
everything was done, or when he was wore to a frazzle,
whichever came first. His belly told him when to eat; anything else he could guess at near enough.

Today, he didn't know whether it was time to eat, time
to go to bed, or time to go crying in his beer. He was just
plum thrown off his stride. If he'd been a horse, he would
have checked his shoes for rocks, his saddle for burrs, and
the pasture for jimsonweed.

As it was, he didn't know what part to check. Leastwise, he did, but he couldn't afford to think about it.

She brought in what she called dinner and Jake had always called supper. First came a platterful of innertube
patches. They were little, they were black, and they were
thin. From the look of pride on her face, you'd have

thought she was serving one of those fancy cuts of beef all gussied up in ruffled britches.

Jake managed a sickly smile.

Next came the sausage. It was a cake, all right. A one-pound cake that had been baked in the oven until it was tan on the outside, pink on the inside, and still oozing grease onto the platter.

"It looked sort of pale," she said anxiously. "I started to put catsup on it, but I wasn't sure you liked catsup on sausage."

"Yeah, come to think of it, some catsup would be right good. You sit, I'll get it."

Judas priest, what was she trying to do, poison him? Give him the bubonic plague, or whatever the hell it was you got from eating raw pork?

She was still sitting there, hands in her lap, an expectant look on her face when he got up nerve enough to go back. He'd forgotten the catsup, but catsup wasn't going to salvage anything; not the meal, not his belly, not her pride.

"Honey, tell me something—have you done much cooking before?"

She shook her head, still smiling. "Rosalie won't let me in her kitchen. She's my housekeeper and probably the best friend I ever had, but she's over eighty years old, because she was past fifty when she started working for Mama and Daddy, but she doesn't like to admit it—she likes to think I can't get along without her, which is mostly true, only I've never had a chance to find out." That last was said sort of wistfully.

"Hmm," was all he could think of to say. Jake was learning a few things about Miss Pricilla Barrington, and he didn't much like it, because what he was learning was getting him all mixed up inside.

She was a nut. She was a screw-up and a royal pain in the behind. Every time she opened her mouth, she stuck in her pink plastic sandal. But it didn't seem to matter. She was so damned sexy she could walk across a room and short out every circuit from here to Fort Worth. Jake had a feeling her heart was even bigger than her cup size, which made her a little too likable—which was dangerous.

And now, dammit, he was either going to have to starve or hurt her feelings real bad.

She held out the platter. He raked off a few of the silver-dollar-size pancakes. They couldn't be as bad as they looked.

"Here, have some butter and syrup while I slice the sausage. Daddy used to have a cook who made this sausage loaf for breakfast that was real good, with applesauce and breadcrumbs and raisins and everything in it. I wish I had the recipe, but I never eat sausage anymore. Rosalie says I need to watch my hips."

He opened his mouth and then shut it again. Wisecracks weren't going to help here.

"Would you rather have molasses? There's a great big jug in the pantry, but it looked sort of moldy around the top, so I thought maple would be safer."

Jake was about to allow as how he took his pancakes, when he took them at all, with butter and a dusting of cinnamon and sugar. Then he put the first one into his mouth and tried to chew.

"Well, maybe I'll have just a drizzle of syrup," he said when he got it chewed and swallowed.

She handed him the vase of syrup and then the platter of sausage, which was when things really started to come apart. Jake was willing to suffer a bellyache for a good cause, but raw pork was another matter. What's more, he couldn't let her eat it, either.

"Prissy," he said. "Honey, have you ever heard about the danger of eating pork that's not real done inside?"

She looked at him, her eyes big as duck eggs.

Then she looked down at the pork, which was just laying there, sort of grayish pink and white except for the edges, which were pale tan.

"It's not done, is it?" she whispered. "I didn't know how long to cook it, but the outside looked done. I thought things cooked from the inside out."

"That's a microwave. Pete doesn't trust microwaves. He says they rob a man of his—well, anyhow, that's why we don't have one. That's, uh, Peter J. Moss." Damned if he wasn't chattering the same way she did when she got nervous. "I told you about him, didn't I? He's this guy who works around here sometimes."

But Priss wasn't interested in any Peter J. Moss, or anyone else. Instead she was remembering her birthday barbecue, when she had given the volunteer fire department nearly a hundred pounds of barbecue—pork, not beef. She'd thought barbecued pork, eastern style, which her mother had never ceased raving over, would be sort of special, so she'd had it flown in.

It struck her then that the fireman who wouldn't allow her back inside her own apartment might have been one of those who'd had to go to the hospital with food poisoning. Could he have been holding it against her all this time, just waiting for a chance to get even?

"Priss? Honey, snap out of it." Jake, a worried frown crinkling the skin around his eyes, came around the table and put his arm around her shoulders. "Are you okay?"

Widening her eyes to accommodate the sudden excess of moisture, Priss drew in a deep breath filled with the mingled scent of horse, man and soap. She shivered, not from the cold this time. Unable to resist, she turned her face to the warm body standing by to give comfort, and found her chin resting on the rodeo buckle he wore on a sweat-stained leather belt.

"There now, sugar, why don't I open a couple of cans of Vienna sausage and we'll smother those pancakes of yours in syrup and have us a feast. I'll even make a pot of coffee—one of those fancy kinds you have to grind yourself in the grocery store. Pete's real partial to one that tastes like Mexican chocolate."

Reaching down with one hand, he found her chin, which was about to drive him crazy, nuzzling his belly the way she was. He tilted it up so that he could look down into those clear, syrup-tan eyes of hers and touched a lineup of freckles on the side of her nose that put him in mind of one of those constellations whose names he could never remember. Orion—Centaurus—Vidalia—something like that. "There now, honey, everything's gonna be just fine. You just weren't used to cooking in a different oven, that's all. Hell, anybody could make a little old mistake like that."

She sniffed, pulled back a little and wiped an arm across her face, bangles jangling like a tambourine player at a tent revival. "Um . . . Jake, I hope you didn't buy that belt buckle of yours thinking it was gold."

He hadn't. He'd won it. He'd won better, but his ex-wife had gone off with anything he'd had of any value at the time, including his bronc-riding and his calf-roping buckles and whatever prize money he'd managed to save up toward a new secondhand horse trailer.

"Because my tongue touched it sort of accidentally. I reckon that sounds awful, doesn't it?"

Her voice was still a little on the raw side, but that was the least of Jake's worries. She'd had her *tongue on his belt buckle?*

Judas priest. Here he'd gone and ridden that damned roan just about into the ground, trying to wear himself out so that he wouldn't be thinking about what he'd been thinking about, and she had to go and *lick his belt buckle?*

"Jake? It's real pretty, anyway. Brass is a nice metal, only it tastes different. Gold doesn't have any taste at all, but brass tastes like—"

"Pricilla."

"Sort of salty and sour, you know, like grape-leaf pickles?"

"Pricilla!" Jake backed away, wishing he still wore his hat, because he needed to adjust something, and he couldn't very well adjust what needed adjusting while she was staring at him that way. If he'd been wearing a hat, he could have tugged the brim down far enough so that she couldn't read what he was thinking. Because he was sure as hell thinking it.

Thinking about how it would be to spend the next few years exploring all the many ways a man and a woman could pleasure one another, and then inventing a few more....

Besides, he'd just as soon keep her attention focused above his belt line.

Years? Had he thought, years? What he'd meant was a weekend. Maybe even a whole week. Jake reminded himself that where women were concerned, he had a short attention span. On purpose!

"Would you, um—like to play a few hands of poker?" Anything, he thought, to get his mind out of the rut it was in.

"Poker? Well . . . maybe, but first I'd better wash these dishes."

"I'll help you," Jake said, which was some indication of just how far around the bend he had come.

Together, they managed to spill salt on the floor, break one saucer, and wet the front of two clean shirts. Jake did know his way around a kitchen, from years of being on his own. Priss knew about as much about dishwashing as she did about cooking.

"Your hair smells good," he murmured, reaching past her to drop a sudsy plate into the drainer.

She buried her chin in the neck of her shirt and concentrated on scrubbing the trademark off the bottom of a baking dish.

"I reckon you go to a lot of parties."

"Parties?"

He shrugged. "Dances. Socials. You know, where folks eat and drink and fool around?"

All the dishes were done, and Priss fumbled frantically around under the billowing suds for something else to wash. He was too close. She could feel his warmth, smell the outdoorsy scent of his clothing—she could even hear the rasp of his breathing. "Yes. Well, that is, I don't go out a whole lot. I could if I wanted to, but—"

She turned around, a look akin to panic on her face. Their eyes met, and Jake reached out a hand to steady her. It was wet. "Priss," he said, his voice deep and slightly unsteady.

"Mercy, would you look at the time!"

Jake couldn't look at anything but a pair of warm brown eyes surrounded by an unlikely thicket of navy blue lashes and a mouth that was just begging to be kissed. His own eyes growing heavy, he leaned forward just as she darted out from under his arm.

He was left standing there like a stump, wanting her so damn bad he could taste it.

"G'night," Priss called out as she dashed from the kitchen. Her voice sounded about two octaves higher than usual.

"Yeah. Right. Thanks for supper."

Sometime before morning another line of storms came pushing up from the southwest, bringing more thunder, more lightning, but little more rain. After one particularly loud blast, Priss sat bolt upright in bed, disoriented—sensing she wasn't at home but unable to piece together the past few hours right at first.

And then she did, and found it impossible to go back to sleep. Finally she crept downstairs and felt her way into the front parlor, to the old, sun-faded, brown plush couch that looked even older than the house, though it was hardly worn at all.

She lay down and pulled a floppy, cretonne-covered pillow over her shoulders against the early morning chill, and slid her bare feet under another one. Downstairs, the thunder didn't sound quite so loud. The drawn window shades helped block out the constant barrage of lightning.

After a while she fell asleep, and it was there that Jake found her when he came downstairs a little later, stiff and groggy, to make coffee.

For the longest time he just stood and stared down at her. She was lying on her side with one knee drawn up, accentuating the curve of her hips, exaggerating the smallness of her waist. With her shoulders crumpled up real small and one hand tucked under her face, she was damned near irresistible. Her hair—that bumper crop of spicy-smelling, hay-colored hair that tempted him almost as much as her body did—had tumbled free of restraint.

It fell almost to the floor, and it was all he could do not to gather it up and—

Yeah, well . . .

Tiptoeing out to the hall, he retrieved a slicker from the rack behind the front door and spread it over her, taking care not to touch her any more than he had to. He lingered another moment or two and then reluctantly let himself out.

Back to the training pen.

Four

While Priss slept on through the dark, dreary morning, Jake put the roan through its paces. He'd taken the stud in after it had near about killed a man up near Nocona. Jake had thought to work some of the trouble out of the roan's system, finish him off some and sell him at the spring sale down in Dallas. That had been over a year ago. Since then, they'd come to know each other pretty well, Jake and the stud. Jake thought he'd keep the horse on for a while longer.

As for the woman, Jake didn't know what he thought about her. As soon as he got a handle on her, she went and moved. Lust was a lot simpler than liking. Easier to understand; easier to deal with.

Jake's history with women went back a long way. It included the usual number of back seat and creek bank episodes, back when he was a fool kid doing his best to live up to a reputation for wildness.

He hadn't exactly earned his reputation—leastwise, not right off. In the first place, there'd been his mother, Jaylene Spencer, who was the daughter of a supermarket manager in a little west Arkansas town. Her mother—not that Jake had ever met either of his grandparents—had been the Sunday school superintendent. After graduating from high school at the age of sixteen and a half—she had always been real smart—Jaylene had set out to Dallas to stay with a cousin and find herself a job.

Her very first day at the El Rancho Beauty Salon where she had taken a position as receptionist and sweeper, she had run into Rex Baker, a stingy, hard-assed oilman from New Hope, who always had his hair and nails done at the El Rancho when he was in town on business. According to rumor, Baker had been a real ladies man back in those days.

At any rate, after less than a week's acquaintance he'd managed to make Jaylene forget everything her mama had taught her about not whistling in public, always wearing a petticoat, and never parting her thighs for a man until she had a wedding certificate framed and hanging over her bed.

When Jaylene had started to get sick at the first whiff of permanent wave solution, she had gone to a doctor, which was when she'd found out she was pregnant. So she'd quit her job, because regardless of the cause, she couldn't stand the smell of permanent wave solution, and moved to New Hope, naively expecting Baker to marry her, even though she hadn't seen him but half a dozen times in the four months since she'd moved to Dallas.

She had gone out to his home to tell him the news, but his gateman had had instructions not to admit any uninvited guests. To which Jaylene had said, "Well, if he doesn't know I'm here, he can't very well invite me inside, can he?''

That argument hadn't set very well with the gateman.

She had finally caught the oilman between his office and his limousine and blurted the news right there in the parking lot, with his driver standing at attention beside the open back door.

Baker had pretended not to remember her, which had just about broken her heart. He had finished the job by telling her that hardly a week went by that some round-heeled floozy didn't try to screw her way into his bankroll. While she was still standing there, big-eyed, slack-jawed and sick to her stomach in the sizzling heat, he had peeled two hundred-dollar bills off a roll and told her she knew what to do with it, and if she ever bothered him again he'd have her picked up for soliciting.

Jake had learned all this the week before his mama had died. She'd done a lot of talking under the influence of the heavy dose of painkillers she'd been taking, and Jake had never been quite certain how much of it was true and how much was the rambling of a dying woman.

The way he saw it, judging from what he'd learned since then—mostly from Big Earline—about all his poor mama had had going for her in those days had been hard luck and pride. She'd headed back to Arkansas to have her baby, only her parents, embarrassed at what the neighbors might say, had sent her packing. She'd come back to New Hope, hoping and praying Tex would change his mind, only of course, he never had. Four months pregnant and still sick as a dog every morning, she had found a job waiting tables at Earline's Kitchen that had since been replaced by Little Joe's Café. She had told Big Earline right up front that she was pregnant, but that she didn't mind hard work and actually welcomed it because it kept her from dwell-

ing on her troubles, so Earline had hired her and she'd
worked until she'd gone into labor.

No, his mama hadn't had an easy life. Jake was ashamed
to admit that as a teenager he'd been embarrassed by the
rusted-out mobile home they'd lived in down in Shacktown, and by the fact that sometimes his mama had stayed
out all night. But she'd always called to let him know she
was all right, and to be sure he'd had his supper. Earline let
her bring home leftover food from the restaurant, and
from the time he was old enough to remember, Jake had
eaten so many meals of pinto beans, cornbread and cole-
slaw that to this day he got indigestion just thinking about
it.

If he had a single regret it was that he hadn't straight-
ened out in time to do more for his mama. Hadn't even
told her that he loved her. Not until she was gone had he
come to realize that she had sacrificed her whole life for
him, giving him a home, seeing that there was food on the
table. She never raised her voice when he got into one
scrape after another, trying to prove himself to a town that
didn't give a sweet damn about a wild young bastard from
Shacktown.

She'd been young, too—not even eighteen when he'd
been born. And pretty, although he hadn't realized it until he'd come across some old pictures. She'd had auburn
hair with a streak of premature gray right in front, and a
smile he remembered to this day. He had an idea she could
have married, but no man wanted a kid with a redwood-
size chip on his shoulder and a real talent for getting into
trouble.

By the time he was twelve, Jake was helping out at home
between bouts of hell-raising—taking every odd job he
could find. He'd always been big for his age, not afraid to
tackle anything for a few bucks. Looking back, it was a

wonder he'd managed to stay out of serious trouble because there was always money to be made if a kid didn't mind risking a little jail time.

Thank God, he had never stepped too far over the line. It would've killed his mama, whose health hadn't been too good from years of working twelve hours a day to keep them in food and him in the clothes and boots he kept outgrowing almost as fast as she could buy them.

Not until she ended up in the hospital did Jake meet his old man face-to-face. Jaylene had been sick in bed for more than a week, claiming it was only a little tad of food poisoning from eating potato salad that had gone off. Jake had stayed home from school to look after her until he'd got scared and called in Earline, who had left work to come down to Shacktown. She had taken one look and called an ambulance, and Jake had followed them to the hospital, so scared he couldn't have spit if his boots were on fire.

They'd put her in the charity ward, which had been mostly full of old folks, whimpering and coughing, spitting and moaning. The whole place had smelled of snuff and antiseptic. He had stuck it out for nearly half a day, waiting for a doctor to come by and tell him she could go home, and then he'd screwed up his courage, eaten his pride, and driven his old pickup out to what was commonly known as Baker's Acres.

To her credit, he didn't think Jaylene had ever told a soul who the father of her baby was. But keeping a secret in a town the size of New Hope was next to impossible. Miss Agnes, Miss Minny and Miss Ethel could ferret out anything, and anything they uncovered was all over town within hours, so Jake had grown up knowing who he was.

He hadn't called ahead, not wanting to give the old man warning, which was why he also didn't give his name at the gate. He'd barged past the gateman, shoved past some high-muck-a-muck in a striped coat, and when Baker had come out into the hall to see what all the ruckus was about, he'd told him to his face that an old friend of his by the name of Jaylene Spencer was lying over at New Hope General in a charity bed, and Jake damn well wanted her in a private room, with a doctor who did more than just walk past her ward and then bill the government.

What's more, he wanted her to have flowers—the biggest batch of roses anyone in New Hope had ever seen, so that everyone would know that Jaylene Spencer was somebody special.

Jake had bought the roses himself. To pay for them, he'd pawned the guitar he'd been trying to learn how to play, which was no great loss to the music industry. He'd found a doctor who had agreed to do everything he could for Ms. Spencer and take his payments on time, but as it turned out, there wasn't much anyone could do except make her last days as easy as possible.

For the first time he could ever remember, Jake had cried when he heard that. He'd gone out and beat the hell out of the door of his truck, denting it so bad the latch never did work right. And then, after learning how to give her the shots she needed, he'd signed Jaylene out of the hospital with the doctor's connivance and stayed by her bed day and night until she'd passed over in her sleep.

She'd had flowers. Jake had sold every stick of furniture in the trailer, knowing they wouldn't be needing it again. He'd bought some flowers with the money and stolen others from the gardens that weren't fenced in. The last couple of days, neighbors had come in to spell him, bringing food and washing Jaylene's bedding, but Jake had stayed right there, sleeping in the cracked plastic recliner he'd dragged into her bedroom.

The day after he buried her in Shady Grove Gardens, he lit out and kept on going, sore of heart, thousands of dollars in debt, and without a single goal other than to get as far away from New Hope as he could in as short a time as possible.

Now, sitting on the top rail staring out at the training pen, Jake absently rubbed his left thigh, which always ached some when a front came through. He'd broken more than a few bones in the following years. He had scars from being dragged, thrown, kicked, gored and stomped, and once he'd come close to losing a kidney when a big Brahma bull had taken a particular dislike to him. The devil had thrown him, hooked him up off the ground by his belt and then shaken him like a feather duster.

The day after he won his first calf-roping money, he'd taken himself a wife. Tammi had been about the most gorgeous woman he had ever laid eyes on, and she'd had a real weakness for cowboys. He'd taken her to bed the first time they'd gone out together, which should have told him something. But he'd been living too fast and hard to learn lessons in those days, trying his damnedest to live down the memories that had followed him out of New Hope, Texas.

Tammi had stuck with him for almost ten months before she'd split, taking everything that wasn't nailed down and leaving him with a bunch of bills to pay when he still hadn't quite managed to pay off all the bills he'd left back in New Hope. He'd been laid up with two broken legs at the time, compliments of a sunovabitch sunfishing paint he'd been counting on to put him in the big money.

Eventually he'd gotten on his feet again, paid off the last of his New Hope bills and got started on the rest. Along the way, he'd finally managed to learn a few basic survival lessons. First off, he'd quit rodeoing and gone into wrangling, which was hard work, but not quite as dangerous. The money wasn't as good, either, but it came in a lot more regular.

Because he had a way with horses—at least those that didn't outright try to kill him, he'd worked his way up, gone bust and then worked his way up again. Eventually he'd paid off the last of his hospital bills and gone into the risky business of horse brokering, where, surprisingly enough, he'd done real good.

Through it all, the ups and the downs, he'd been driven by one goal—to be bigger, meaner and richer than the man who had sired him and then refused to acknowledge him.

Along the way he had learned another valuable lesson: never set store by possessions. Anything a man could possess, he could lose a damn sight quicker. Which was one of two reasons Jake had never bothered to fix up the old house after he'd bought the spread nearly six years ago, the other being that the horse barns were more important. Any money he had to spare went toward improving that end of the business.

Still...maybe, he thought, watching another bank of purple clouds move in from the southwest—maybe a little paint wouldn't hurt. A few rugs—some furniture that hadn't come over on the ark.

And a syrup pitcher, he added, grinning as his thoughts turned back to the woman he'd left sleeping on the parlor couch.

He wondered if she had any idea that she was enjoying the hospitality of a bona fide bastard. The world had gone around a few turns since he'd been born. A little thing like illegitimacy didn't cut much ice these days, even in a small town like New Hope.

One thing he did know—her old man, if he'd still been alive, would have gelded him first and then run him out of town on a rail for fooling around with his little girl.

Still grinning, Jake eased his aching left leg down a rung or two and then jumped the rest of the way. He reckoned it was time he went back and woke up his houseguest. Then he'd better round up Petemoss and see about wiring up the new dryer before she took a notion to tackle it herself.

The first thing Jake noticed when he walked through the door was that the house smelled different. It could have been any house in the world and he could have been blindfolded, and he still would have known there was a woman close by.

It wasn't her perfume, although he had noticed that right off back at the baby store. Good stuff. Not overpowering like the five-bucks-a-pint perfume the ladies in waiting at New Hope's unofficial bordello over on Bent Street wore.

"Priss?" Funny, he'd never noticed the way voices echoed in the high-ceilinged old house.

The clatter of heels drew his gaze toward the stairs. She had managed somehow to dry her clothes—leastwise, she was wearing them again. There was a brown streak up one side of her pink knit top. "I have to go to town," she announced.

"Right now?"

"Right now." Loaded down with her purse and her assortment of parcels, she was wearing full warpaint and the same roadkill hairdo that had been the second thing he'd noticed about her the first time he'd seen her. When she stopped about three feet away, he took the time to admire the way her eyes looked surrounded by navy blue lashes about a foot long, and the pale, metallic pink of her lips.

Inhaling, he appreciated the soft corn-tassle scent of her perfume, mingled with the smell of soap, scorched cotton and something else that never failed to set his juices to flowing.

"I told you I forgot to bring my hair-dryer?" Priss continued. "I almost never got all my hair dried! I thought maybe you might have one, but I looked and couldn't find one. Oh, and by the way—you're nearly out of deodorant."

Jake blinked at that. "It's a good thing you noticed. Then I reckon I'd better go clean up some."

"You don't need to change for my sake. If you'll just drop me by the apartment, you can come on back home."

"They're letting you move back in already?"

Her gaze slid away, and Jake lifted one dark eyebrow. She couldn't lie worth a hoot.

"By the time I get to town—I mean, there's no real reason why I can't—and by the way, Jake, while I think of it, I owe you for three toll calls. The garage said they picked up my car yesterday right after you called."

"I told you they would," he said blandly. She was squirming. Jake discovered that he liked setting her at a disadvantage. He'd take any edge he could get.

"Yes, well—they said it'll take at least a week, so my insurance company's going to find me a decent loaner to use in the meantime."

"You're welcome to stay on here, you know. I could find you something to drive."

Her chin came up. She had the damnedest little chin. It was the kind that started out to be pointed, changed its mind at the last minute and ended up soft and round, with a shadow of a dimple.

He knew from experience it wasn't near as soft as it looked. Like the roan stud, she had her stubborn little ways.

"No, thank you," she said in that tea-party accent that had irritated him so much the first time he'd heard it. Now he found it amusing. He found *her* amusing. And touching. And irritating.

Not to mention arousing.

If he'd been smart, he would have stuck to watching her from a distance, letting his imagination off the leash for a little while and then going on about his business. He had a sneaking suspicion that from now on it wasn't going to be quite so simple.

Jake reached for the wooden chest Priss had left on the hall bench at the same time she did. Their arms collided and Priss jumped back, looking as if he'd branded her with a hot iron.

What would she do, he wondered, if he was to sweep her up in his arms and kiss the living daylights out of her, the way he'd been wanting to do ever since he'd gotten his first good look at her?

Scream, probably. Scream and hightail it down the road. With her bags flapping and her crazy plastic shoes, she'd probably break a leg before she even reached the cattle gate.

"Sorry," he said, trying to keep the amusement and frustration out of his voice. He'd been feeling a lot of that in the past twenty-four hours—amusement and frustration.

"It's my fault. I've always been sort of clumsy."

"Honey, face it, you're no clumsier than I am. It's just that we strike sparks off one another." He could tell from her expression she knew exactly what he was talking about. Not that she'd ever admit it.

But then she went and did. "You mean, you felt it, too? It's crazy, isn't it? I mean, we don't even like each other," she said earnestly.

Was she waiting for him to deny it? It wasn't that he didn't like her, he just wanted her so damn bad there wasn't a whole lot of room for anything else.

Her eyes clouded up and Jake thought, Oh, hell.

"But don't feel bad about it," she said with a shaky little smile that wouldn't have convinced a tombstone. "It's not your fault. I've just never been real good at making people like me."

He could only stare at her. She said it as if she really believed it, which made him want to shake some sense into her. Fortunately, he knew better than to lay a hand on her again, what with all the electricity in the air.

"Let's go, if we're going," he muttered. "I've got to get back here in time to feed up."

On the road south, neither of them talked very much. Jake came to the conclusion that Priss was insecure, which surprised him because he couldn't figure what the devil she had to be insecure about. She'd grown up rich, hadn't she? And legitimate? It sure as hell couldn't be on account of her looks.

At first he'd thought she was obnoxious and a little bit nutty, in spite of being about the sexiest woman he'd ever laid his eyeballs on, but now he didn't know. He just didn't know....

As for Priss, she didn't know which she dreaded more—seeing her own place all grimy and soggy from smoke and water, or spending another minute in the company of a man who kept her so bumfuzzled she couldn't open her mouth without saying something stupid. She'd told him the truth—except for the kids at the hospital and Rosalie and Faith and Sue Ellen, she never had been real good around people, especially around men. But with Jake, she was hopeless. The more she tried to make a good impression on him, the more she ended up sounding like a fruitcake.

Priss knew she wasn't stupid. She'd graduated from college with a liberal arts degree, which didn't seem to be worth a whole lot in today's marketplace, but she wasn't really stupid.

The trouble was, whenever she got flustered, her tongue outran her brain. All she had to do was watch Jake Spencer walk toward her with his hat pulled down and his belt buckle drawing her attention to where it had no business being, and she started chattering like a cageful of squirrels.

Clutching her mama's wooden silver chest on her lap, she made up her mind to call Rosalie and ask her to please come home right now. She would make it up to her later, but right now she needed her in the worst kind of way, and not just for cleaning up the mess in their apartment, either.

As to that, they were going to have to come to some sort of an understanding about who did what from now on, but that could wait. All her life it had been Rosalie who dried her tears, kissed away her hurts and generally kept her out of trouble. When she'd grown up and started dating—not a whole lot, but some—it had been Rosalie who warned her that most men were lazy, trifling scoundrels who were usually up to no good, and that a girl had to watch out to see that they didn't sweet-talk her out of her crown jewel before she could even think to cross her legs.

Between Rosalie and her daddy, Priss thought a little sadly, it was no wonder she ended up having to go to a sperm bank to get herself a baby.

And that was another thing she was going to do as soon as she got settled back into her apartment—find out when Miss Agnes wasn't going to be on duty at the sperm bank and finish what she'd started. And this time she wouldn't let herself be talked out of it!

Five

"Now, don't forget," Priss said minutes later as they turned into the parking lot of the Willow Creek Arms. "I gathered up all the laundry and washed everything, but it's all still out on the clothesline, so if you're missing anything, you'll know where to look."

Jake said nothing.

"You don't have to thank me. It was no trouble—I mean, it seemed like a shame to have that great big old tubful of water just for my handful of clothes, only I couldn't get the dryer to work, so I had to hang everything outside, but then I had to dry my things in the oven, because I couldn't very well wear your shirt and long underwear home—"

"Petemoss's longhandles, not mine."

"What?" She fiddled with the seat belt, which had a tendency to slide up over her bosom and catch her in a stranglehold around the neck. "Anyway, I knew better than to try to dry your silk shirt in the oven. Silk's delicate, even wash silk.''

Still Jake said nothing. He didn't know what wash silk was, but the label on his shirt said Dry Clean, so he damn well dry-cleaned. It was a hell of a lot easier, anyhow. Maybe he ought to take to dry cleaning his jeans and work shirts.

Priss hurried to fill the silence. ''I do all my own hand laundry, but Rosalie insists on doing everything else. I do know how to use a washing machine. I mean, what's to do? You put stuff in, dump in some soap and turn it on, right? And when it's done, you take it out and pop it in the dryer. Only, like I said...''

Jake looked as if he might have a stomachache. She knuckled him on the arm to get his attention. ''Jake? Is something the matter?''

''Darlin', you remember what you and your friend were talking about in that baby store yesterday just before you tripped over my feet?''

Yesterday? How was she supposed to remember yesterday when he was calling her ''Darlin''? Eddie had called her sweetie—he called all females between the ages of fourteen and forty-five sweetie. Darlin' was different. She'd never been anyone's darlin'. Oh, she'd been called sugar and honey before. Most folks around New Hope called people sugar and honey. It didn't really mean anything.

But ''Darlin''' drawled in that soft, raspy baritone of Jake's, made her insides shiver. ''What...what am I supposed to remember?''

''About wantin' a baby?'' Jake prompted.

She yanked her seat belt away from her neck again. ''That was a private conversation,'' she said stiffly.

"In a public place," he reminded her. "But, honey, Miss Agnes was right. Maybe you're not quite ready to take on a baby."

She looked so hurt he started to take back his words, but dammit, it was the truth. She *was* useless. Pretty as a picture—about the sexiest female who ever filled out a pair of jeans—but totally useless. "Now, look—don't take this the wrong way, but maybe you ought to look around for a husband before you start making any babies."

At least, he thought, a husband would see to it that she didn't throw out the baby with the bathwater—or toss it in the dryer when it got wet. That any woman her age could be so flat-out helpless amazed him, it surely did. By the time she was Priss's age, his mama had been holding down a job, growing her own tomatoes, chilies and onions in a two-by-four plot behind the trailer and trying to raise a kid who was hellbent on kicking over the traces.

"That's a rotten thing to say. Just because I didn't dry your clothes—"

"Honey, I'm only trying to do you a favor. This Rosalie of yours—did you ever think she might not want to take on the raising of a youngun at her age? You said she was getting on in years."

"You think I can't do it by myself? You think just because I have a housekeeper—just because my mother and father sent me east to school—that I'm spoiled and useless and—" Her voice faltered. "Is it because of the sausage?" A look of horror dawned on her face. "It *is!* You think just because—"

"Now, honey, calm down. It's not the sausage, and I never said you were useless. All I said was—"

"You didn't have to say it. You think I couldn't pour myself a glass of water if I was dying of thirst. You're just like everyone else, you think that just because Daddy had money, just because I've always had Rosalie, I can't do a blessed thing for myself!''

"No, I don't. I didn't say anything about—"

"Well, let me tell you something. I don't have all that much money anymore. I have to watch what I spend just like everyone else, and I'm even studying—"

"So how come you can afford to hand out two hundred and seventy bucks, times a whole bunch, on a whim?"

"It wasn't a whim, it was my birthday present to myself. I saved up for it, and it's none of your business. And besides—what were we talking about?"

With a reluctant grin, Jake told her. "Money. Babies. Rosalie."

"Yes, well, how do you think she'd feel—Rosalie, that is—if I took over all her work? She'd be the one to feel useless, and let me tell you, there's *nothing* worse than feeling useless!" Her indignation would have been funny if her eyes hadn't been blinking so hard he could feel the breeze all the way across the seat.

Turning in at the showy entrance to the Willow Creek Arms, Jake did his best to ignore those flapping, inch-long, navy blue lashes that should've looked all wrong with her whiskey-brown eyes, but didn't.

After wheeling into an empty slot beside a heating contractor's van, he cut the ignition, turned to face her, and gathered both her hands in one of his, trying not to notice the contrast between his scars and calluses and her soft, perfectly manicured fingers. "Now listen here, you want to calm yourself down before you blow a gasket. Chances are, you're not going to be able to do more than go inside and grab a change of clothes—and maybe a decent pair of shoes."

"I'm staying."

"Mmm-hmm. But just in case, don't you think—"

"It's my apartment. I pay the rent. If I want to stay, then nobody's going to keep me out."

Jake couldn't figure out whether she really believed it or was just trying to crank up enough courage to storm the fort. At that moment, he could well believe she was her father's daughter, and he'd never even met H. T. Barrington.

He knew the type, though. He dealt with them all the time, buying and selling their horses. Some of them were real fine folks. Some weren't worth cow flop, but he went on buying and selling their horses because he was good at it, and because he could make more in commission on a few good sales than he'd made in all his wrangling and rodeoing years put together.

And every sale he made brought him that much closer to his long-term goal.

Priss opened the door and slid out before Jake could stop her. Moving stiffly, thanks to the weather and too many years spent getting his carcass busted—getting thrown again this morning by that damned stud hadn't helped, either—he eased out from behind the wheel, and caught up with her just as the super came out to meet them.

"Miss Barrington, you can't go inside yet. I'm real sorry, but the fire chief would have my scalp."

Priss pointed up to the second-floor balcony of her apartment. Through the sliding-glass door, a man on a ladder was clearly visible inside. "That's my dining room chandelier he's messing with! How dare you tell me I can't go in when you let a stranger inside my apartment?"

How dare you? Jake couldn't remember the last time he'd heard that quaint expression. Just in case, he eased up beside her, ready to grab hold of her arms if she started swinging. "Come on, now, honey, be reasonable," he placated.

"Reasonable! People I don't even know are free to mess with my chandelier and I'm not even allowed to go inside?"

"Honey, you have to understand—"

"They're bonded, Miss Barrington," the super said anxiously.

"I don't care if they're cast in bronze, I want them out of my house, and I want *you* out of my house, and I want—I want—"

Her voice wavered dangerously, which was when Jake decided it was time to take a stand. He turned to the super. "Now, why don't you just explain to the lady what's going on in there, friend?" Priss moved closer and Jake wrapped an arm around her waist and hooked his thumb under her concho belt in case she tried to bolt. Times like this, a short rein was called for.

The superintendent started gabbling like a turkey trying to outrun a coyote. He had more to say than Jake wanted to hear about leaks and cracked drywall, about ceiling fixtures that were full of water that had to be dried out and rewired, and walls that had to come down to give access to a whole bunch of stuff.

By the time he got around to the problem with the vent pipes, Jake had stopped listening. Priss's brows were down, her chin was poked out, and her mouth looked ready to start spitting bullets. Either she was about to blow, or she was about to cry, and Jake didn't know which he'd rather deal with. All he knew was that all hell was fixing to bust loose unless he stepped in and cooled things down.

He turned to the super. "I reckon we're going to have to disoblige you, friend," he said gently. "You've got my word that we don't aim to cause any trouble, but the lady needs a few more of her personal belongings, and I'm here to see that she gets 'em.''

Whatever protest the man was about to make died after one look into Jake's level, steel-gray eyes. "Well . . . okay, but you'll both have to wear hard hats," he conceded grudgingly.

"Fine. Bring 'em on." Jake removed his Stetson and carefully walked back to place it on the front seat of his truck. Handed two construction hats, he settled one on his own head, then considered Priss's shaggy, haystack hairdo. "Easy now—looks like we might have to squash your hair down a mite to get this thing on your head."

Enough was enough, as far as Priss was concerned. Snatching the bright blue hardhat out of his hands, she jammed it on her teased and spritzed hair without regard to the result, and said, "Come on, if you're coming. I haven't got all day!"

It was more than two hours before they headed north again. The space behind the front seat was stacked high with luggage, tote sacks and half a dozen framed watercolors, which Priss had insisted on dropping off at a framer's to be cleaned up, rematted and reframed.

Jake waited, drumming his fingers on the steering wheel while she went inside, wondering just when his brain had started to mildew.

A scrawny little chair had to be dropped off at a refinisher's shop—he insisted on carrying it in himself, in spite of her insistence that she was perfectly capable of carrying a vanity chair.

A vanity chair? What the hell did she do with that—sit down and practice being vain?

The funny part was that in spite of her looks and her background, he didn't think she was vain at all, which sort of surprised him, now that he thought about it.

Back in the truck, she called her insurance agent, discussing at length the effects of water on feather cushions and linen draperies, which led Jake to share with her his philosophy about living close to the bone.

"I've never set much store by fancy furniture and such. See, the way I figure it, it doesn't make much sense to load yourself down with a lot of nonessentials. Anything you can own, you can just as easily lose, so if you don't own too much, you can't lose too much."

If Priss appreciated his words of wisdom, she didn't say so.

Jake shrugged. "Now, I'm not meaning to sound unhospitable or anything like that, but do you think you're going to be staying long enough to use up three big suitcases full of clothes?"

"Some of them are Rosalie's things. She wouldn't want me to leave them where strangers could paw through them. And if you don't want me, just say so. I'm sure I can find a room at the hotel."

The finishing school accent was back on duty. He'd noticed that it came and went, depending on how comfortable she was feeling.

"I'm sure things have thinned out by now," she said.

"Think so, huh? You know what day this is?"

She blinked at him, and once more Jake felt the draw of whatever spell it was she'd cast on him with those whiskey-colored eyes of hers. "Friday?"

"Friday the what of what?"

"Friday the . . . second of July?"

"Which means tomorrow's the third, and Sunday's the—"

"I can count, for mercy's sake!"

"Okay. Then what happens every Fourth of July?"

"The parade, the barbecue, and the square dance. Oh, shoot!"

Priss had planned to be out of town over the Fourth because she always cried at parades and ruined her mascara—march music affected her that way. And barbecue reminded her of that awful mess last year on her birthday. And as for the dance, every time a man asked her to dance, and surprisingly enough, many did, she found herself wondering if he was only interested in the money he thought she still had, or if he was one of the boys who'd been scared off by her father years before and was wanting to try his hand at seducing her now that the old man was out of the picture.

All things considered, Priss had never cared much for the Fourth of July celebrations in New Hope. At least in Dallas, whenever a man paid her any attention, she was reasonably sure he wasn't thinking about *who she was* and the money H.T. was supposed to have hidden away where the IRS couldn't find it until the statute of limitations had run out.

She heaved an enormous sigh. What a miserable mess. Maybe she ought to move away and start all over somewhere else, where no one had ever heard of Horace Barrington and his Canadian mining operation and his fancy offshore investments and his trouble with the IRS.

"Rainbow," Jake said, breaking into her dreary train of thought.

"Where?"

He pulled the truck onto the shoulder and rolled down his window. Reaching across the seat, he drew her over until the brim of his hat nudged her hair, and pointed.

"Right over yonder, see? One foot over by that grain elevator, the other over near Denton County."

Priss saw it and breathed softly in wonder, feeling a ticklish little flutter that might have been caused by such transient beauty or might have been caused by the scent of Jake's skin, the laundry-soap-and-horse smell of his clothes. If he used a cologne, it was a subtle one.

Or maybe he hadn't felt the need to gussy up just for her.

"Who's Eddie?" Jake asked quietly, his breath stirring tendrils of hair against her throat.

"What? Who?" She watched the rainbow shimmer and begin to fade as another layer of clouds moved in.

"This Eddie guy who married Grace Something-or-other. He a particular friend of yours?" New Hope was the kind of town that was small enough so that everybody knew everybody else by sight, but big enough so some of them never actually met.

"Oh, for heaven's sake." Priss twisted around to glare at him and found herself entirely too close for comfort. Sliding back over to her side of the seat, she made a production of refastening her seat belt.

"Were you engaged?"

"No, we were not engaged! If you must know, I went out with him a few times—all right, more than a few times. But it was never serious." She had only hoped it would be.

"Uh-huh."

She sighed as he pulled back onto the highway and headed north. "He works at the bank. His daddy's president, and Eddie's working his way up from the bottom, trying out all the different positions."

Trying them out with every single teller, she thought bitterly. For a man who wasn't particularly handsome, nor even all that intelligent, Eddie had a way of teasing that made a girl forget what a worm he really was.

It had certainly worked on her, even though Eddie had been one of the two boys who had shown up for her birthday party all those years ago, clogging the pool filter with birthday candles and crepe paper hats and teasing her unmercifully about her breasts, telling her she ought to try Band-Aids, as they'd fit better than the bra she was wearing.

The creep had come within an inch of teasing her right into his bed! Fortunately, she had come to her senses at the last minute.

At least, she thought it was fortunate. At the rate she was going, she might never know.

"Rain's all cleared up," Jake observed. "Want to stop off at Buck's and get some barbecue to take home for supper?"

"You're the host." She had long since lost her appetite for barbecue.

"You're the guest."

Priss sighed heavily. "Maybe we could pick up a cookbook from somewhere? I *do* know how to read."

Jake shot her a quick look, which she met with a wry grin of her own. "I guess that wasn't too tactful," he said. "I, uh, heard about the thing with the barbecue a couple of years back."

Grimacing, Priss replied that everyone in Collins County had heard about the barbecue. "At least I learn from my mistakes. Last year I settled for committing a federal offense by stuffing things in mailboxes."

"And this year you're planning to celebrate by getting yourself a, um—what you might call a personal donation."

"Oh, Lord. How much did you hear?"

"Near about everything, I guess."

"Yes, well . . . sometimes I talk too much."

He chuckled. "You do have a way with words. Don't worry about supper, honey—Petemoss'll round us up something."

Petemoss did. The old man met them at the front door, a calico apron wrapped around his ample waist. "So ye brung 'er back. She the one got all the clothes wet an' left 'em to rot?"

Jake started handing luggage inside the door while Pricilla did her best not to slink away in shame. "I told you to hook up that dryer before we both ran plumb out of clean clothes. Maybe now you'll get around to it."

"Humph! D'ye get eggs?"

"No, I didn't get eggs."

"I told ye we needed eggs! Sausage's gone, too. Stole right out o' the icebox." The old man glared accusingly at Priss, who was beginning to come to a slow boil.

"I used the egg and I ruined the sausage. If you'll tell me how much I owe you, I'll pay you back right now." She whipped open her purse and reached for her gold-bound, lizardskin wallet.

"You want to try hitting the rodeo circuit again?" Jake asked, his tone of voice quietly lethal.

The old man snapped back, "No more'n you do. Ain't a-goin' to, neither. If you don't want me to cook and clean no more, I'll jest find me a bed in the poorhouse. Be obliged if ye'd forward my mail."

Jake removed his hat and raked a hand through his hair, leaving it standing in three separate windrows. He sighed. "Priss, this is Mr. Peter J. Moss, from up Montana way. He's a first-class rodeo clown and a third-rate cook, and he's got the manners of a hungover grizzly bear."

Priss didn't know whether to offer to shake hands or to run for her life.

"Pete, this lady is Miss Pricilla Barrington." The ex-rodeo clown's shaggy white eyebrows pole-vaulted all the way up to his hairline. "She's going to bunk here for a few more days until her place gets fixed up again. If it's going to strain your goozle too much to keep a civil tongue in your head, then you can damn well sleep in the barn again."

"No, please—" Priss stepped forward and laid a hand on the old man's arm. All three of them stared down at the inch-long, frosted-pink fingernails on Pete's faded, no-color shirtsleeve. "That is, I ought to thank you for the use of your underwear, Mr. Moss—"

"Huh?" the man gawked.

"Oh, hell," Jake swore softly.

"But I can leave right now," Priss continued. "I really don't want to be a nuisance. Jake insisted—that is, he didn't actually insist, but I sort of—well, we ... You see, my loaner wasn't ready, so—"

"Priss," Jake said with exaggerated patience. "Kindly shut up and let's start hauling your gear upstairs while Pete rustles up some supper. That okay with you, Pete?"

The old man hooked his thumbs under his apron sash, the effect probably not as threatening as he supposed. "I done made chili."

"Good," Jake said flatly. And to Priss, "Pete makes right tolerable chili."

"It's got to be better than what I did last night." Priss's slow smile had a remarkable effect on both men. "Maybe before I leave you could show me a few tricks so that I don't poison myself if I ever have to do my own cooking again," she suggested, which made the old man swell with pride until the buttons strained across his chest.

Jake shook his head in disbelief. Another good man shot down. Was she even aware of her power?

God help us all, he thought as he watched her pick up two bulky tote sacks and wobble her way upstairs. Those shoes were going to have to go. For his sake, if not hers.

Six

Saturday. Priss had missed two readings at the hospital. She had hoped to make it up tonight, but she didn't know how she could manage to get herself into town. Her car was going to take at least a week to repair, and the loaner she'd been promised was not yet available. She thought several unflattering things about a town the size of New Hope that had only a single rental agency.

It had to be the holiday weekend. The Fourth was always a big event in New Hope, and when it fell on a weekend it was a three-day whoop-de-do. People came from all around, and every available vehicle was turned into a float for the parade.

Jake had mentioned finding her something to drive, but then she'd be even more beholden to him than she was now. The thought made her nervous for reasons she didn't care to dwell on.

"Ants in yer pants?" Pete asked, and she nodded. That about described it. Jake had left early in the morning for Fort Worth to see a man about a horse.

Actually, it was about twenty horses, which, according to Pete, who was showing Priss how to boil coffee, Jake would then arrange to have transported to the Bar Nothing, where he would pasture them, finish them off and sell them in the fall sale.

And she didn't miss him, she really didn't, Priss told herself. Pete was surprisingly good company, now that they'd agreed on the fact that Priss was a total disaster in the kitchen and that Pete could cook circles around any chef in New Hope, from Antonio's famous kitchen magician to Sue Ellen at the diner.

"Sue Ellen does bake an outstanding lemon meringue pie, though," Priss opined, out of loyalty to a woman she admired more than almost anyone she could think of. Except, perhaps, Rosalie, who'd been orphaned at seven, gone to work at nine, and supported herself ever since, never once losing faith in her God, her church, or herself.

"You ain't never tasted my bread puddin'," Pete told her, to which Priss could only reply that no, she never had.

"Coconut, raisins an' pineapple juice. Makes it real tasty. I'll bake one fer supper tomorrow night. Jake'll be home by then, I reck'n."

Priss hadn't asked. She had sort of hoped he'd be back later on today, but then, she hadn't the least notion of how long his business would take. Or what other business he had in mind to do. He could have a lady friend in Fort Worth. He could have a dozen of them. He was single. He was the kind of man any woman with a viable hormone in her body couldn't help but respond to. Goodness knows, Priss had enough trouble keeping her head anchored on when he was around.

Which was one more reason why she needed to find herself some wheels and another roof and get out of Jake's way as soon as possible.

"Is that eggshell you just put in the coffee?" she squawked.

"Yep. Settles the grounds." Pete took down one of the heavy white crockery mugs and poured her a sample. "Now this here's the way to make real coffee, not that sissy stuff folks makes nowadays in one o' them electric pots.'"

Priss took one cautious sip, grimaced, diluted it half and half with milk and added two heaping spoonfuls of sugar. "Interesting," she said.

By the time the sun had dried up most of yesterday's rain, leaving only a few shallow puddles in the deepest ruts, Priss was aching in places she had never ached before. She had blisters on her hands from wielding a mop, and more than once she'd had to knead cramps from the calves of her legs. Pete operated the machinery, but after a few trips upstairs to carry yesterday's laundry, strip the beds, carry the freshly laundered linens back up and make the beds again, she changed into her new lizardskin boots. By midmorning she was barefooted, her frosted-pink toenails a close match for the blisters the new boots had worn on her little toes.

Pete, claiming kitchen duties, disappeared after giving Priss a list of things that still needed doing. Not until she had worn herself to a frazzle while he "Whomped up a feast fit fer a rodeo queen," did she discover that he had merely put a pot of beans on to boil, slipped into the office and spent the next few hours in the recliner, watching soap operas on the tiny television set that had been half hidden behind a stack of letter files.

They ate lunch, which Pete called dinner, in the kitchen amid a sinkful of dirty dishes and an ironing board piled high with shirts and pillowcases. Pete had promised her an education, and if she survived, Priss supposed she'd be educated.

"Cook don't never wash the dishes," he declared, rising from the table and hitching up his belt.

"Oh? Who does?"

"You."

"Oh. Well . . . I can do that. Where's the dishwasher?"

The grizzled old rodeo clown nodded in her direction. "There she be."

By dinnertime, which on the Bar Nothing was called supper, Priss had learned how to spray-starch and iron a pillowslip so that it was as crisp as a sheet of vellum. She had even learned how to iron a man's shirt after a few minor mishaps. There was an iron-shaped scorch on the back of one of Jake's chambray work shirts, and as for the black silk . . . well, it had looked sort of tattered, anyway, even before the hot iron scrunched up the piping on the yoke and ate a hole in the fabric.

Amid the noisy Fourth of July celebrations, which would go on all weekend, Jake left Fort Worth with a signed contract in his pocket that should translate to a tidy commission, depending on how many potential buyers he could interest in the Trowbridge stock. It was top quality breeding stock, but a lot would depend on the market. He had intended to stay over, make a few calls, look up a certain widow he hadn't seen in a couple of months, and maybe set off a few fireworks of his own.

Instead, he found himself back on the highway headed north, knowing he was riding into trouble, calling himself seven kinds of a fool. All day Priss had been busting up his concentration. For near onto three hours he'd sat across the table from Ben Trowbridge, sharing steaks, drinks and cigars, with Ben talking horse and Jake doing his damnedest to stay one step ahead of the wily old pirate.

Then, right in the middle of a discussion of prospects, prices and pedigrees, he found himself gazing off into space, picturing a certain well-filled pair of jeans, a certain heart-shaped face with a pair of big, whiskey-brown eyes and a pouty mouth...wondering how she would taste.

Trowbridge was no fool. He might look a little slow, but his beady little eyes saw entirely too much. Again he went over the particulars while Jake did his best to focus his mind on the tricky business of horse trading.

He'd been lucky to get away with his shirt on his back, much less a halfway decent contract.

Damned female. Jake reminded himself that she was off limits. It didn't help.

He reminded himself that all he ever wanted in the first place was the temporary use of her body for a little wholesome, mutually satisfying sex between consenting adults, which he figured was a perfectly natural craving.

But that was before he'd found out that she was the kind of woman he'd avoided like tick fever all his life. Barrington's daughter out of some high-rumped female from back east.

Jake knew exactly where he'd gone wrong. His first mistake had been following Priss into that baby store and tripping her up just to get his hands on her. His second had been taking her home with him. As for his third mistake...

He wasn't going to make a third mistake. No way. He was going to get her out from under his roof if he had to drive her all the way to Dallas and book her a suite in the best hotel in town. He'd like to think it was a matter of honor, but he had a feeling that by now it was down to a matter of survival.

A burst of fireworks lit up the darkening sky, punctuating his irritation. Jake told himself that at the advanced age of thirty-five, with his life finally on the right track, the last thing he needed was to tangle with a snooty, high-maintenance female with fog for brains. No matter how sweetly she was put together.

Sex, he told himself, was a legitimate human need. Like vitamins. Jake tried to be conscientious about looking after his health. He ate right. He allowed himself a single beer each night, and mostly, he stayed away from the hard stuff. Mostly. He got enough sleep. He made it a point not to get himself thrown more than twice a week. When it came to sex, he wasn't as quick out of the chute as he used to be, but then, as a man grew older, he learned to be a mite more discriminating.

The trouble came when he started thinking beyond sex. Thinking of ways to finagle a smile instead of ways to get into a lady's bloomers.

While sporadic fireworks lit up the sky in the distance, Jake swore softly, turned off I-35W onto 380 and headed east. When, he wondered, had life got so dangblasted complicated?

Priss had already made up her mind to forget about Jake. The last thing she needed in her life right now was some hardscrabble wrangler who didn't even own a dishwasher or a microwave—who had all the finesse of a bulldozer. Whose slightest touch set off quivers that started in her belly and ran all the way down to her toes. Lord have mercy, she might not be the smartest woman in Texas, but even *she* knew better than to grab hold of a live wire.

Which was why she flat-out refused to ask another leading question, refused to listen to another Jake-story from the old man he had rescued from the streets and given a home and a job.

The trouble was, Pete enjoyed having an audience too much to stand on ceremony. While Priss washed the dishes, he told her all about the first time Jake had taken top money in the bronc-busting division. It had been a small rodeo, the competition mostly small-town boys trying to prove their manhood.

Nevertheless, Jake had been proud as punch. To celebrate, he'd stood a couple of rounds, blowing off about maybe tackling Calgary next time around. Still basking in glory, he'd gone off to check into the fanciest hotel in town and soak some of the dirt and hurt out of his carcass.

In no time at all he'd come roaring back into the saloon, demanding to know what lousy jackass had been messing around in his bedroom, fooling around with his blankets—even leaving a chunk of candy on his pillow just to let him know they were smart enough to bust into a locked hotel room without getting caught.

Pete shook his head, chuckling at the memory, but Priss had no trouble at all picturing a younger Jake Spencer, unused to the turn-down service in a first-class hotel, getting his back up over what he thought to be a practical joke. The man had more defenses than a porcupine.

Neither Priss nor Pete was expecting him before morning, which was probably why Priss had let her hair down after supper, both literally and figuratively. They were dancing. At least, Priss was dancing and Pete was keeping time to the beat of the radio with two tablespoons. He claimed to have played professional spoons with a bluegrass group once when the rodeo circuit was on the eastern swing.

"Are you two having fun?" Jake drawled from the doorway. He was staring at Priss's hair, which had finally surrendered to the laws of gravity.

She froze in mid-shimmy, hands over her head, fingers in snapping position. "We weren't expecting you tonight," she said breathlessly as Pete rammed the spoons into his shirt pocket and hobbled over to silence Brooks and Dunn.

"How'd it go?" the old man asked, giving Priss time to pull herself together.

"Not bad."

"See ye come away with yer scalp."

"Yep."

"Heard tell that Trowbridge bunch is slicker'n owl droppin's." Pete cackled. Priss looked from one man to the other, feeling like an outsider—a feeling that was all too familiar.

"Got anything to eat?" Jake asked, taking off his hat to run his fingers through his hair. He looked tired. Or as Pete had said about her earlier that evening, he looked like he'd been rode hard and put away wet.

"P.J. here, she'll fix you up a bait o' beans an' cornbread. Plenny o' coffee left over."

"P.J.?" A glint of amusement flickered briefly in Jake's shadowed eyes.

"Go 'long, gal, heat 'im up some o' them beans. Medium high, an' don't fergit to stir 'em."

"Never mind," Jake said. "I had a steak for dinner. That'll hold me."

He was still standing in the doorway, staring at her so intently she wondered if the label was sticking out of the neck of her shirt. "Should I go ahead and heat the beans anyway?" she asked uncertainly.

"Nah, Jake hates beans. Mama bean-fed 'im till he was near 'bout growed. Oughtta see this young'un dance, boy. She c'n twist an' shake prettier'n that little sunfishin' paint that busted your two front legs that time up in Tulsa. Y'ought to dance with her. Doc Bender, he says a man that don't get enough exercise, his joints seize up on 'im so he can't hardly move."

"Does that apply to jawbones?" Jake asked dryly.

Chuckling, the old man sidled out of the room, pausing to switch on the radio again. Priss stared at Jake, wishing she had gone to bed right after supper the way she'd intended to. She'd been so tired she could hardly move, but Pete had pulled a long face and started talking about how lonely it was for an old man with no family of his own.

On the radio, Hal Ketchum was singing a lonesome, bitter ballad. Outside, she could hear the occasional burst of thunder. It sounded almost like cannonfire—not that she'd ever heard actual cannonfire.

"Do you...want to dance?" she asked, wondering even as she spoke where the nerve to ask had come from. She could just imagine how it would feel to sway in his arms, to rest her cheek against his shoulder, moving in slow harmony together....

"Thanks, but I don't dance."

"Oh." She felt her face grow warm, and he shook his head.

"Can't, is what I mean. I'd like it right much if I knew how, but I'd just trample all over those pretty pink shoes of yours."

They both looked down at her feet, which were bare. Priss tried to think of something intelligent to say, and then Jake crooked a finger at her. "Come on outside a minute. "I got something to show you," he said.

The first thought that popped into her head was that he'd found her a loaner. In her relief, she never even stopped to wonder how he could have driven two vehicles home at once.

Flustered, she hurried after him, and Jake hooked a hand around her arm and pulled her with him to the edge of the porch. Neither one of them remembered to unhook. "Look over yonder," he said, and she looked.

"Where?" All she saw was his truck and the empty horse trailer that was parked next to the shed.

"Watch the sky over town."

"The sky? The pink glow, you mean?" Puzzled, she lifted her gaze. The night air was cool, laden with the smell of grass, dust, horse and honeysuckle. There was no sign of lightning, in spite of the thunder she'd thought she heard.

And then suddenly there was a starburst—and then another one. "Fireworks!"

Jake, grinning down at her, looked as proud as if he'd arranged the whole display for her benefit. "Pretty, huh? Thought you didn't care much for the Fourth," he teased, his voice quiet against a background of insect noises and distant explosions.

"Only the parades and the dances. I've always loved the fireworks. I used to watch from my bedroom window when I was a little girl."

"I used to watch from the roof of the place where we lived."

And from the poolroom. And the garage where the rougher element gathered most nights to shoot craps and drink beer. Once from the backstairs landing of a local prostitute. She'd been his first. The fireworks had been an anticlimax.

His arm slipped around her shoulder. It was getting to be a habit, being close to her this way. Jake told himself it didn't mean anything. He was just being friendly. It was just the way folks were around these parts.

He remembered what she said about not liking to be touched, but then he remembered the way she nuzzled up against him every time he put his arm around her. Like a wet kitten curling into a warm pair of hands.

"There—watch right there," he said gruffly, pointing as he leaned down to align his sight with hers. He caught a faint hint of her perfume, but mostly she smelled of soap, shampoo and scorched cotton.

Priss wrapped her arms across her chest and tried to concentrate on the fireworks display instead of the man who was standing entirely too close. A large circular starburst appeared out of the blackness, looking like nothing so much as a sparkling crystal chandelier. She held her breath as it sloped over toward Denton County and slowly twinkled out.

Moments later she heard the distant, muffled boom she had earlier mistaken for thunder. Feeling a familiar lump in her throat, she braced herself. *Not now. Not now, silly!*

She heard again her mother's voice. "Oh, for heaven's sake, Pricilla Joan, must you carry on that way? It's so common."

But common or not, Priss had never been able to hide her feelings. They spilled over at the most embarrassing times. How could she explain why watching a marching band made her cry when she didn't understand it herself?

Or watching a big airliner taking off and disappearing into the clouds.

On certain days of the month, she could even manage to choke up watching a Greyhound bus pull out of the terminal.

Priss gave a ladylike snort, and Jake leaned down. Without quite knowing how it had happened, she was in his arms, her back leaning against his chest. "Did you say something?" he murmured.

She took a deep, steadying breath. Her eyes burned. Her nose was stopped up. She reached behind her to dig out her handkerchief and her knuckles brushed Jake's groin. He stiffened. She groaned. Another flowerburst appeared in the sky, followed by the same deep, distant boom. "I'm sorry, I didn't mean—that is, I wasn't—"

She sniffled and without releasing her, Jake dug a handkerchief out of his own pocket and shoved it into her hand. "Blow," he said, and blow she did.

"I'm sorry. I don't know why I have these silly spells."

Jake didn't know, either. All he knew was that women were about as predictable as a Texas twister. And about as dangerous.

"I knew an old man once who used to cry over the Three Stooges," Jake said. He didn't. He'd only heard about him thirdhand, but he thought it might make her feel better.

"I'll wash your handkerchief for you. I—the dryer's working now. Do you want starch, because I know how to iron, too."

"Don't go to any trouble," he told her, wondering why he didn't order his feet to get him the hell out of there before it was too late.

Probably because of the way her hair tickled his chin, and the way her firm little bottom was nuzzling him right where it counted.

"It's like bombs bursting over a battlefield, isn't it?"

"Come again?"

"The fireworks. Bombs bursting in air. You know. Like 'The Star Spangled Banner'?"

"Now that you mention it, I reckon it might look like that." If he'd thought about it at all, it would probably have reminded him of rodeo parades. Or the time he'd overdosed on beer and chilidogs at the annual celebration and woke up on the back stoop of the Baptist church with the granddaddy of all bellyaches when somebody set off a bunch of firecrackers right beside him. He'd been thirteen at the time.

Priss shrugged, and Jake's body registered every nuance of movement. When his arms tightened imperceptibly, she burrowed a little closer. He was more than willing to oblige. Now all he had to do was figure out a way to keep his enthusiasm under control.

She sighed, and he wondered if she was thinking what he was thinking. "You know, when I was a little girl," she said softly, "Mama told me about her great-granddaddy, who was named Walter Raleigh Gilbert Ambrose, who was in The War, and about his great-grandfather—I don't know how many greats—who fought the British in northern Virginia and died a hero. D'you think maybe that's why marching music always makes me want to cry? Thinking about men like that, who went off to war? Only that wouldn't explain the planes or the buses, would it?"

"The planes and buses. Uh-huh." Jake tried in a half-hearted sort of way to make sense of what she was saying, but his mind was on more important matters, such as turning her around in his arms and kissing her until her knees buckled.

And then, maybe making arrangements to get together later, after she was settled back on her own turf, so they could meet on more or less equal terms.

Equal. Right. Baker's bastard and Barrington's little princess.

And then she turned in his arms. Propping her forearms on his chest, she peered up at him just as another rocket burst in the air, and said, "You know, I get these feelings sometimes. Mama used to get so put out—"

"I know what you mean, darlin'. I get these feelings, too."

So what the hell—he kissed her.

Fireworks. That about described it. And quicksand. Jake knew he was in trouble the instant his mouth touched hers. She was soft as a cloud, but so warm…so sweet, like whiskey and honey.

And willing. She reached up and wrapped her arms around his neck like a pea vine climbing on a hogwire fence.

She kissed with her mouth closed, which was, somewhat to Jake's surprise, a turn-on. She wasn't real stubborn about it, though. With a little effort on his part, she opened to him, and then the fireworks commenced bigtime. Jake felt like a rocket all ready to launch.

A hundred years later, he came up for air. Panting, he rested his chin on the top of her head and tried to make sense out of what was happening. "Prissy? Honey?"

"Oh, my goodness," Priss said softly. "I didn't mean to do that." Kissing was no new experience. She'd been kissed before, lots of times. Well…maybe not lots of times, but enough to know that there were kisses, and then there were *kisses*.

Evidently, the power had been off those other times. This time, it had been switched on. She felt as if she must be glowing in the dark. "I think maybe I'd better go to bed," she whispered.

"Yeah, I think maybe that would be a good idea," Jake said.

Priss was a little disappointed that he agreed so readily, but it was probably for the best. What with all that had happened to her since yesterday, she hardly even recognized herself.

Dreamily massaging revitalizing cream into her face and throat a little while later, she wondered why a man Jake's age had never learned to dance. Everybody knew how to dance. She'd had dancing lessons before she was out of grammar school.

And then she wondered how he felt about children. What was it Faith Harper had said about him? That he'd been married?

Priss brushed her hair slowly, trying to picture the kind of woman Jake might have married. And if he had been married, then where was his wife? Because, try as she would, she couldn't imagine any woman who was lucky enough to capture a man like Jake Spencer ever allowing him to get away. He was nothing at all like the boys she had dated at college. Or the men she had dated since then. He wasn't polished. In fact, in his own way, he was almost as big a social misfit as she was, if for an entirely different reason.

She wondered what his reason was. Remembering the way he had looked in the Baby Boutique, surrounded by stuffed animals and tiny furniture, she wondered if he had ever thought about having a family.

Little boys, who could follow him around while he did whatever it was that he did.

Little girls who could wear blue jeans and get dirty and yell and climb trees, and have puppies and eat in the kitchen and never once have to think about *who they were*.

Seven

The early morning sun hit him right square in the face, which had never happened before. It didn't improve his mood. Jake scowled down at the kitchen table, which was covered with a cloth for the first time since he'd bought the place furnished off old man Holloman six years ago.

What he should've done was manufacture another trip into town. He'd lain awake half the night trying to figure out what to say to Priss after making a fool of himself out on the front porch. Smelling her hair. Feeling her soft backside pressed up against his hard frontside. She had to have known what she was doing to him. One touch and he'd been hot as a branding iron.

Dammit, he should have known she'd be trouble the first time he'd seen her out at old man Barrington's auction. Instead, he'd watched for her every time he'd come to town, and then gone home and fantasized about her while he lay awake at night after his bedtime beer.

Finally, he had worked up his nerve to speak to her, and now...

Doggedly, Jake concentrated on the mound of scrambled eggs on his plate, studiously not looking at the woman across the table from him. He should never have followed her into that damned boutique place. Never have spoken to her. Never have looked into those big, clear, whiskey-brown eyes.

She wasn't like any other woman he had ever known, and not just because she looked at the world through a slightly cockeyed lens. Faith Harper liked her. Faith was a nice girl. Which meant that Priss was probably a nice girl, too, and Jake didn't have all that much use for nice girls. He went in more for the rowdy, weekend type. Weekend women didn't have families. Hell, some of 'em didn't even have last names.

Priss had a grandfather a bunch of generations back who'd fought in the American Revolution. Jake didn't want to know that kind of stuff about her. It made her too real. Too close.

Jake had never met his own grandfathers. Never even seen a picture of them. All he knew about his mother's father was that he was supposed to be an upstanding citizen in some little town in west Arkansas, but he'd gone and turned his back on his only child when she'd gotten into trouble. Which didn't say a whole lot about upstanding citizens.

As for the paternal side of his so-called family, Jake figured Baker had probably sprung up in the middle of a cow flop one night after a hard rain, like some kind of fungus.

All in all, Pricilla Joan Barrington and Jake No-middle-name Spencer didn't have a whole lot in common. Not that it mattered.

Hell, he'd even forgotten to drink his beer last night, he'd been so caught up in picturing her standing in the doorway, waiting for him to come home. Picturing her in his bedroom. In his bed.

Priss cleared her throat, bringing him back to his senses. "I'm sorry about your shirt," she announced.

He reached for the salt shaker and concentrated real hard on oversalting his eggs.

"I mean, about scorching it. It was the first thing I ironed, before Pete showed me about the settings. I, um— I could buy you a new one..."

That and a new hat. At the rate she was going, he thought, she was going to owe him big time. He'd see how good she was at paying her debts.

No he wouldn't. He might not be a gentleman born and bred, with ancestors, a college degree and all the trappings, but he did have his standards. Taking advantage of a woman who was under his protection, so to speak, wasn't going to happen.

But dammit, he didn't want to know all that stuff about her family, or the way she felt about marching bands. He didn't want to hear about the ancient housekeeper who ought to be put out to pasture, but who was still working because some blonde with big hair and an even bigger heart wanted to make her feel useful.

All that was supposed to matter to him was the way Priss looked in tight-fitting jeans.

And out of them.

Hearing her draw a deep breath, Jake braced himself. She shoved back her plate untouched and squared her shoulders, and it occurred to him, not for the first time, that shoulders were a highly underrated part of a woman's body.

"About last night," she said, brushing crumbs off the tablecloth—which was just one of the changes that had happened around here since Jake had brought Priss home with him.

"Forget it," he growled, and watched her head come up. If she'd been a horse, her ears would be flat on the back of her head. As it was, he didn't know whether to back off or move in.

"I'll forget it just as soon as I even the score between us."

Even the score? Hell, so far nobody on either side had scored. If he knew what was good for him there wasn't going to *be* a score.

"I smudged your best hat, and don't tell me it's just some old thing you wear mucking out the stalls, because Petemoss told me how much you paid for it and how careful you were not to bruise the felt."

"Pete can go—"

"And your shirts. After I scorched the one you're wearing, I turned the heat down, but it was still too hot for your wash silk, so it made a hole in the yoke, but if you want my opinion, the shirt didn't look all that good even before I ironed it. There's a lot of real cheap silk around these days. Your shirt practically fell apart in my hands when I pulled it out of the washer."

Jake choked on a piece of bacon. By the time he had recovered, she was standing beside him, getting ready to whack him on the shoulder blades. The way his luck was running, he'd end up in traction if she did.

"And you might as well know I broke two plates yesterday. If you had a dishwasher, those things wouldn't happen. Oh, and Pete would really like to have a TV set in the living room so he wouldn't have to watch his soaps on that teensy little thing in your office. You could move the chair into—''

''Whoa. Just hang it up, will you?'' Jake stood and shoved his chair under the table. When he turned around, she was too close and he stepped back, bumping his legs on the oven door, which had been left open to cool down after Pete had baked biscuits. ''Dammit, woman,'' he growled, ''We need to get a few things straight.''

''I agree.'' She crossed her arms and waited.

''First off, I liked things just fine the way they were around here. I like my table turned around the other way so I don't get a face full of sun in the morning. I like my cotton shirts dried in a dryer, and not ironed.'' Truth was, he didn't give a hoot in hell how his shirts were laundered, as long as they were reasonably clean. Clothes had never been a real big priority, but she didn't need to know that. ''I like my silk shirts dry-cleaned, the way the Good Lord intended, and—''

''But wasn't it— I mean, it looked like—''

Jake ticked off another item on his fingers. ''I like my best wool suit pants—'' his *only* suit pants ''—dry-cleaned, not shrunk all out of shape. I like my sausage fried in half-inch patties, my pancakes served with butter and sugar and cinnamon, and I like my—''

''I thought they were acrylic.''

''My *pancakes?*''

She hadn't bothered to paint her face before breakfast. Jake was fascinated by the sweep of her sand-colored lashes, and the way they twitched when she blinked. Which she was doing a lot of. ''Aw, hell, you're not going to cry again, are you?''

Up went those militant little shoulders again. It was all he could do to keep his hands off. ''I never cry,'' she said coolly.

"Right. Just like you don't like being touched."

Tactically, it was the wrong thing to say. He knew it the minute the words left his mouth. Using the same tone of voice he'd used on many a skittish horse, he said, "Look, why don't we just call it square? A couple of shirts—hell, that's no big deal. Pete says you've been hustling your buns—uh, bones—around here, cleaning up, changing beds, washing dishes and all. We'll just call it even. Is it a deal?"

She shook her head. The haystack hair, which he'd been astounded to learn took her nearly an hour to arrange so that it looked like she'd just crawled out of bed, slid a little more to the leeward. "Barringtons always pay their debts," she declared.

Which elicited a lifted eyebrow from Jake. The way he'd heard it, her old man had died owing twice what he was worth to the IRS and various other creditors.

She must've noticed his skepticism. For all the lady looked so soft, she was sharp as a tack. He knew just what she was thinking. She was thinking she knew just what *he* was thinking. What the whole town, if not the whole state of Texas, had thought when old Horce T. had kicked off. There'd been enough publicity.

It wasn't Jake's style to grovel. On the other hand, he'd have cut out his tongue before he deliberately hurt her feelings. Frantically, he wracked his brain to come up with some way to defuse the situation. "Hey, did I tell you I got asked to go to the dance the other day?"

Her expression was neither interested nor encouraging. So he tried harder. "Thing is, I've always had two left feet. That's why I didn't want to dance last night. But now I'm thinkin' maybe if I had somebody to give me a few pointers, maybe show me how to aim 'em in the same direction, I might give it a try sometime." He risked a quick glance, wondering if she would take the bait. A bead of sweat trickled down his neck and puddled at the base of his throat.

"You want me to *teach you how to dance?*"

"Well, not what you might call dance, but at least how to shuffle around a dance floor without tripping over a lady's feet."

Against all odds, her eyes began to sparkle. The corners of her mouth twitched. Jake started to protest that it wasn't all that funny when he remembered how they'd met. He started to chuckle and she did, too, and then, damned if they weren't wheezing all over the kitchen.

"The place was so jammed full of stuff—"

"I didn't even see you standing there until—"

"And then you came barreling down the aisle—"

Priss gave one last shuddering gasp, wiped her eyes, and looked up at the strikingly masculine man in the worn jeans, the scarred boots, the big brass buckle and the scorched shirt. He was most definitely *not her kind of people,* but she wished with all her heart that she was his—*kind of people,* that was.

Or maybe just his, period, she thought with a sense of wonder not untouched with fear.

"I do know how to dance," she said. "You might've noticed that there are a few things I don't do very well, because I've never had much practice, but I had dancing lessons practically before I even got all my permanent teeth."

"I never did," Jake vowed solemnly.

"Get your permanent teeth?"

"Have dancing lessons. Don't get too big for your britches, young'un," he teased, and Priss felt a glow start in her toes and work its way up to her cheeks.

"We could start now," she suggested, but Jake shook his head.

"Finish your breakfast. I've got some work to do for the next few hours. After supper tonight we'll find you pair of steel-toed boots and we can try a little do-si-do-in'."

He gave her the kind of smile that left her feeling totally defenseless. Afraid to speak—afraid she'd say something stupid—Priss followed Jake to the front door and watched him move across the barren front yard in that lean, loose-jointed swagger that looked almost as if he were compensating for a limp.

She wondered just what there was about him that affected her so strongly. Because something purely did.

She wondered if he was like all the males her father had warned her against from the time she'd turned thirteen—after either her virtue or her money.

Which might be a problem, because she had too much of the one and not enough of the other.

Turning to go back inside, she caught sight of the dead tomato plant in the plastic container and frowned. A lack of interest in landscaping was one thing. Priss could understand how two men living alone, probably not earning a whole lot, might skimp on the frills, but keeping a dead plant around was just too much.

By noon she had swept and mopped the front porch, talked Pete into repairing the swing, and dragged an ugly square table from an unused room at the back of the house out onto the porch. A handful of wild daisies and some decorative seedheads made an attractive bouquet. She arranged them skillfully in the syrup vase and placed it on the table.

Stepping back, she admired her handiwork and told herself that perhaps she had hidden talents after all. All her life it had been drummed into her head that there were people who were hired to decorate houses and landscape grounds, to design and make clothes, or to decorate a cake—and then there were those who were in a position to hire them. And she should consider herself fortunate that she was among the latter.

Instead, she had considered herself useless. And frustrated.

Taking classes in horticulture at the local community college, which was what she'd really wanted to do, had been out of the question. Obediently, she had earned herself a liberal arts degree from her mother's college in Virginia. The wildest, most exciting thing she had done during her four years there was to audit a class in French literature without written permission.

It had been mostly in French, which she didn't speak, and exceedingly boring, but because she wasn't supposed to be there, she had stuck it out.

Her first real rebellion had come after she had graduated, when she'd stated her intention of looking for a job in Dallas. From the reaction, it was as if she had threatened to go to work waiting tables at a topless bar and grill.

So she had fumed and waited, meanwhile taking over a small portion of her father's huge estate and turning it into a Japanese garden, Texas-style, with boulders, raked gravel, a bench, and a variety of cacti.

Gradually she had started dressing to please herself instead of wearing the well-bred little classics her mother insisted on buying her. The more her parents had protested, the more she'd go out of her way to defy them. It had given her, for the first time in her life, a feeling of power.

By the time her mother had been diagnosed with a rare, inoperable form of cancer, her father was already in deep financial trouble, if the increased consumption of Scotch whiskey and the steady parade of grim-faced accountants was anything to go by.

Priss had drifted through the following period like a ghost in her own home, afraid to speak above a whisper, feeling grossly inadequate, ignored by her father and shunted out of the way by a regiment of nurses whenever she tried to sit with her mother.

It was during that awful time that she had renewed her old friendship with Faith Harper and Sue Ellen Rainey. Sue Ellen was years older than Priss and had been divorced three times, but she was one of the wisest, kindest women Priss had ever known.

It was Sue Ellen who was responsible for Priss's volunteering at the hospital in the children's ward. When a daughter of one of her regulars had come down with a staph infection, Sue Ellen, in her usual kindhearted mode, had been anxious to visit the child, to sit with her while her mother was at work. Rather than possibly ruin Sue Ellen's business by trying to fill in at the diner, Priss had offered to visit little Callie Ann, herself.

Thus she had discovered a whole new world where the few things she really did well counted for something.

Jake stayed down at the training pen a lot longer than his presence was required. Evidently, Pete had passed the word to the two other hands that there was a woman up at the house. He took a ribbing he could just as well have done without.

About half-past noon, the two hands, Rico and Joe, broke for dinner and headed home. They were both married, with half a dozen kids between them, both ex-cons who'd showed up broke and hungry, looking for work about the same time Jake had been getting started. After sizing them up, he'd taken them on, worked with them to fix up a couple of bungalows on the other side of the creek, and never once had cause to regret it.

Because he wasn't ready yet to deal with the situation up at the house, Jake stayed out all day. By late afternoon he was hot, tired, dirty and hungry, having taken delivery of the Trowbridge lot, looked them over, and worked with a filly who'd taken an immediate dislike to her new quarters. A couple of the mares were past prime breeding age, but he figured he could sell them to one of the dude ranches he supplied, and made a mental note to call.

Then, because nothing else that day had presented him with any real challenge, he had saddled up the roan and gone a few rounds.

"You and me, boy—I reckon we're still fighting old battles," he murmured as he rubbed the stud down and turned him into the paddock.

Jake didn't know much about the horse's past, other than that he'd had more owners than Jake had trophies and that he'd tried to kill at least one of them.

Jake's own past, he knew about. Having decided a long time ago that his chances of making a go of another marriage were about as good as his chances of coming in top money at Pendleton, Cheyenne or Calgary, he had his future all mapped out. It didn't include a permanent arrangement with a woman.

He could tell right off when he parked the truck in the shade of the shed roof that she'd made some more changes. For one thing, the swing was no longer dangling from a single chain. For another, she had dragged a table out onto the porch and set a bunch of weeds on it. Damned if it didn't look right nice.

Pete's vegetable garden was gone. The old coot had read this piece in the Fort Worth paper about patio gardening, and thought he'd give it a try on a small scale. Jake had known all along from his mother's limited gardening that it wasn't going to work.

Pete and Priss were in the front parlor again. Evidently, supper was going to be an event tonight. Jake only hoped Pete was doing the cooking.

Or if he wasn't, that they weren't having sausage.

"Come on, now, P.J., I done it just the way you said." He heard Pete's plaintive voice as he headed upstairs to wash some of the real estate off his carcass.

"The knife blades are supposed to be turned this way, not sharp edge out, and the—"

Grinning, Jake shook his head. Next thing he knew, she'd have him wearing a necktie to supper. Which he would no doubt spill gravy on, and she would toss in the washing machine and then burn a hole in with a hot iron.

Twenty minutes later he came back downstairs, his hair still wet from the shower, his chin nicked in a couple of places where he'd scraped off his late afternoon growth of beard.

He'd put on a clean shirt, clean jeans, and his best boots, which was all the concession he was going to make. Give the woman her head and she'd be serving him a saucerful of those little pretty things he'd heard her telling Pete about, while Pete balanced a cup of tea on his knee.

Supper was chicken-fried steak, mashed potatoes and gravy and canned peas, which was about his most favorite meal of all, except maybe for Little Joe's Five-Alarm Chili.

It might as well have been dried oats.

The table had been spread with what he suspected was a sheet. Pete's ugly dishes sparkled like the finest china, and she had used her own silverware instead of his mismatched stainless steel.

But it was the woman herself who plumb squeezed the wind right out of his barrel. She wasn't wearing jeans. Instead, she'd dressed up in something soft and floaty that reminded him of sunset on a dusty day. Layers of colors. Pinks, oranges, and a shade of brown that was a perfect match for her eyes.

The shape of her body didn't really show, but Jake had never been more aware of what was underneath all those wispy layers than he was when he stood in the doorway and watched her lean over to light a candle.

Her hair, as usual, was piled like loose-stacked hay on top of her head, with little bunches of it sliding down around her ears. It just plain drove him wild with wanting to wind it around his fingers.

Sure enough, she served him some of those little square things that looked like samples of layer cake that had been left out in the hot sun too long. "Petits fours," she told him. "They're frozen. Pete and I drove in to the Winn-Dixie."

"That's spelled p-e-t-i-t-s," Pete put in smugly. "It's French." He'd gussied himself up like a cheap hoodlum on a Saturday night in a purple satin shirt and a bolo set off by a chunk of fake coral.

"I know how to spell, dammit," Jake grumbled.

"Yeah, you spell near 'bout as good as you read."

"Which is a damned sight better than you write."

"More coffee?" Priss put in. She claimed it was something called espresso. It tasted more like Pete's pan-boiled coffee after the third day, but Jake held out his cup. Anything to keep from what he was afraid was going to come next.

Which was dancing. A tape player had been playing Vince Gill and Allison Kraus real low while they'd eaten supper. It occurred to Jake that he didn't even own a tape player. That must've been some shopping trip, he thought sourly.

Except for the table and chairs, the furniture had been shoved back against the wall. A cloud-soft voice came from the tape player.

Talk about a man knotting his own noose. What the hell had he been thinking about, challenging her to teach him how to dance? He already *knew* how to dance.

Leastwise, he knew how to wrap his arms around a woman and hold her up real close while the music played. That was just your basic he-ing and she-ing. He'd learned how to do that kind of dancing before he'd ever left New Hope High.

But if she had any notion of getting him out in the middle of the floor to twist and shake his butt and wave his hands in the air, then she was flat out of luck.

Inevitably, the moment came. Priss stood and nodded to the tape player while Jake wondered if he should show her his scars and plead incapacitating injuries. Like the complete absence of a brain.

"Pete, you want to turn the tape over while I clear up these dishes?"

Jake could feel the sweat forming on his back start to trickle down to his waist.

"Nah...you go 'long and get started showin' the boy how to dance. I'll take care o' this mess. But just fer tonight, mind ye. Cook never—"

"I know. Cook never washes up afterward."

"You're a-learnin'," he said.

"I'm trying," she replied with a smile that could melt pig iron.

As for Jake, he was long past the age of learning anything. If he'd needed proof, it was the woman holding out her arms to him, daring him to put himself in her hands.

Eight

Once in a small rodeo down near Amarillo, Jake had drawn a palomino that had earned the name of Goldie From Hell. Before he was even out of the chute, he'd known why. He'd lasted four seconds. The minimum was ten. The record on Goldie was six.

He figured this time he might even last seven, but not much longer.

"You put this hand right here," Priss instructed, taking his hand and placing it on her back, slightly above the curve of her waist. Jake curled his fingertips into the shallow valley of her spine and took a deep breath. Inhaling her perfume, he started to sweat.

"Now. Take my other hand—like this." She demonstrated, and he wished she'd given him time to wipe his palm off on the seat of his pants first. She looked so serious and so damned sweet. "Now, when I count three, slide your left foot to the left. One, two—like this."

Separated by an arm's length, they slid to the left, they slid to the right, and Jake slid deeper down a slippery slope that he recognized but refused to put a name to. He tripped over his own feet a couple of times, but he didn't trip over hers even once.

Priss wondered if this had been such a good idea. She had always liked music, had taken years of piano lessons before her teacher had given her up as a lost cause. As a musician, she remained only a talented listener.

But for once the music failed to capture her imagination. The lyrics went right over her head. She was deaf to the melody, her senses too full of the man who was holding her.

Somehow the arm's length had shortened to a few inches. Her sense of touch registered the rocklike shoulder where her hand was resting, the leathery palm enclosing her fingers. Her sense of sight soaked up every detail of his face, from his wide, thin mouth with its full lower lip, to the tanned hollows under his high cheekbones, to the squint lines at the outer corners of his silver-gray eyes.

He was wearing a crisp, light cologne. She smelled the clean detergent smell of his shirt and the faint hint of some exotic essence that was pure, unadorned Jake Spencer. There was a scar, barely noticeable, high on his left cheek. Another one on the edge of his jaw. Pete had said he'd rodeoed in his younger days. She thought he must not have been very good at it.

Although there was that belt he always wore...

He'd won it in a calf-roping event, Pete had said. Or was it bronc-riding?

"Priss?"

But then, she couldn't picture him failing at anything he attempted. He was too tough. Too determined. Too—

"Priss. Honey?"

He was entirely too— "What?" She blinked, suddenly aware that she was pressed up against his body and he was holding her there with both arms—and that he was sexually aroused.

Oh, for goodness sake. She gulped, forgot to breathe, remembered to try, and strangled.

Jake patted her on the back, but the pat turned into a caress, and that didn't help matters at all. "Honey, the music's stopped," he said. "Are you all right now? You want me to turn over the tape or put a new one in?"

The music?

Oh. They were supposed to be dancing.

Carefully, Priss disengaged herself and attached a bright smile to her face. "Yes. I mean, no—that is, I think we've done enough for now. You're getting the hang of it, don't you think so? All you have to remember is step, slide, step, slide—one, two, three, four."

"Yes, ma'am. Step, slide."

His eyes—had she called them silver? They were the color of old pewter. There was a high flush on his cheeks, as if he might be coming down with a fever.

"Jake, were you out in the sun today without your hat?"

"My hat?" His voice sounded raspy.

He stared at her in a way that made her wonder if she'd worn too much makeup. He was no longer touching her, but it didn't help. The whole front of his body was permanently imprinted on hers.

"Hat," she blurted. "Oh, and by the way, it's club soda. The fizzy kind. I remember reading it in a magazine once, or maybe it was Hints from Heloise, only I've never tried it—I don't know if it works on mascara."

Jake continued to stare at her as if she'd burst out speaking Swahili. Maybe she had. The way he was watching her made her nervous, and when she was nervous, she invariably started babbling, and when she babbled, there was no telling what might come out.

Then, right out of a clear blue sky, he started swearing. Priss thought at first it was something she had done—or said. It usually was. But when he grabbed her by the shoulders and hauled her into his arms, and then started kissing her, she was pretty sure it wasn't just to shut her up, because...

Oh, my...

He kissed with his mouth and his teeth and his tongue—and his arms and his hands, and—oh, his body. Straining against her, grinding against her—his big brass belt buckle catching in her floaty gauze dress and tugging at the neckline. Or was that—

It was his hands. And then his lips. Her head fell back so that he could trace the tendon at the side of her neck with his lips, and then he was nudging her earrings, licking the lobe of her ear, and it tickled in places that weren't even faintly connected with her ear...

Jake felt behind him for the couch. His legs bones, busted and mended too many times over the years, felt about as stable as wet spaghetti. If they were about to give out on him, he needed to know it, because while he wanted nothing more than to be lying beside her—or on top of her—damned if he wanted to do it on the floor.

"Let's not rush into anything," he muttered, wanting desperately to rush into something.

The music had ended. Jake still couldn't dance, but somehow he had managed to waltz her over to the couch, where he eased her down and collapsed beside her. He allowed his arm to settle accidental-like across her shoulder, but he held back on making his move. Once he did, it had to be good, and he figured he'd better wait until he could trust himself to kiss her again without disgracing himself.

Damn. He was as nervous as a snake eating razor blades. Jake the Rake, the man who had once bragged that he'd won more fights, drank more beer and had more women by the time he was sixteen than any man in Texas.

It went without saying that he'd also told more lies.

God, it was a wonder he'd survived to adulthood. He sure as hell didn't deserve it.

Back off, man. This isn't one of the girls down on Bent Street you're dealing with.

It had been so long since he'd had any dealing with a woman like Priss—not that he ever had; not with a woman like Priss—that he didn't know quite how to handle it.

Hearing a funny buzzing sound in his ears, he thought he must be finally falling apart. His past must be catching up with him.

Then he realized she was humming.

Humming?

Leaning back, his arm still around her shoulders, Jake peered at her through narrowed eyes. "Are you okay?" he asked, sort of worried.

She laughed. Man, if ever a guy didn't want to hear laughter, it was when he was about to make his big move.

"I'm trying to remember how it went...you know? 'Mama-as, *don't* letcha *babies* grow up to be cow-bo-o-oys...'"

She was as tone deaf as he was, bless her sweet little—

Yeah, well. It wasn't her heart he was interested in, Jake reminded himself as he carefully disengaged his left arm. Good thing he'd remembered in time. This dancing business, what with the music and that fancy dress of hers—if a guy wasn't careful he could get snookered in so deep he plumb forgot his priorities. If there was one thing Jake was flat-out set on doing, it was keeping his priorities straight.

He cleared his throat. "Much as I appreciate the dancing lesson, honey, I'm afraid I'm never going to be much of a threat to old whatshisname—the cat in the black-and-white suit in those old movies."

"Fred Astaire," Priss filled in for him. Actually, she was glad the music had ended when it had, because she'd come close to forgetting what they were supposed to be doing. She could've stood there all week, secure in his arms, swaying to the music, feeling warm and loved and sexy. It was getting so she couldn't be around him for two minutes without wanting to curl up in his arms.

And then he'd kissed her, and it had seemed like the most natural thing in the world until the old doubts began to creep in. Could her father have been right after all? That it was the Barrington bank account that was the big attraction?

If that was the case, poor Jake was clean out of luck. The only part of her father's estate she'd inherited was a small annuity, and she'd already overdrawn her quarterly allowance sending Rosalie to Dallas with gifts for all her nieces and nephews, plus enough blood pressure medicine to last her until she got back home.

If, on the other hand, it was her virtue he was interested in, that was even worse. Because as embarrassing as it was to admit, she still had it. At the advanced age of twenty-nine, she was still depressingly whatever that latin phrase was that meant a virgin. She'd overheard it at the sperm bank. They'd made her answer a lot of nosy questions about her periods, her blood type, her income and her love life—things that were nobody's business but her own. And then she'd filled out a long questionnaire, turned it in and waited, which was when she'd overheard the woman in the white coat talking to someone in the office, and then Miss Agnes had come in and things had gone from bad to worse, and she'd stormed out, spitting mad, and headed to Faith's to buy toys for her children.

"Priss? P.J.? Honey, are you asleep?"

"What? Of course I'm not..." She realized she was stiff as a board, both fists knotted in her lap. For one brief moment she allowed her head to rest on his shoulder. "Jake, I'm sorry. Once in a while I forget there are other people around and go off somewhere in my head."

Forcing herself to relax, she settled back against the hard cushion, relishing Jake's warmth and the comforting feel of his arm across her shoulder. As angry as she'd been at the time, she supposed they couldn't just give babies to anyone who walked in off the street wanting one. At least that part of it was over. Next time maybe they'd give her one of those little fertility kits and tell her when to come in again. She'd already been reading up on how to use it and all.

"Go off somewhere in your head, huh? Sounds good to me."

He smiled that nice, crinkly-eyed smile and then they both fell silent. For the next few minutes, the only thing to be heard in the square, ugly room was the occasional creak of old boards cooling after the day's sun and the sound of their own breathing, which had slowed considerably.

As a child, Priss had learned to disappear into her own world when the real world came at her too hard and fast. As an adult, she sometimes still did. Her fourth-grade teacher had once called her a solitary child. The description had caught her fancy.

Priss had enjoyed dramatizing herself at that age. She'd been, by turns, a foundling left on the wrong doorstep by mistake; Princess Priscilla, stolen by Gypsies and rescued by a masked man, and Elizabeth Taylor in *National Velvet*. Because fantasies weren't required to make sense, hers seldom did.

Somewhere along the way, the solitary child had turned into the lonely woman, but by then there wasn't much she could do about it. The harder she tried to be like everyone else, the more of a mess she made. At least Faith and Rosalie and Sue Ellen had accepted her the way she was. And of course, she had the kids at the hospital.

"Penny for 'em?" Jake drawled.

There was no coffee table. They had scrunched down so that their legs were stretched out in front of them, crossed at the ankles. Jake's were longer than hers. The boots he was wearing, while not new, were expensive. Having three pairs by the same bootmaker herself, Priss recognized the quality.

"Nice boots," she said.

"You were thinking about my *feet?*"

"Not your feet—your boots. I have some almost like them. Not as big, that is, but with almost the same design."

Jake fingered a piece of her skirt that trailed across his thigh. "I've never seen you in a dress before," he said.

"We only met day before yesterday—or was it the day before that? Way out here in the country, I lose track of time."

"It was Thursday, but I'd seen you around town a few times before that. You were always wearing jeans."

"Everybody wears jeans. I hate to be conspicuous."

When he didn't reply, she peered up at him and caught him grinning. "What?" she demanded. "Jake, what are you laughing about? Is it because for any woman not to be conspicuous these days, she'd have to be wearing maternity clothes? Honestly, did you ever see so many people getting pregnant? It's a regular epidemic.''

That hadn't been exactly what he'd been thinking, but Jake let it pass. If she had any idea how conspicuous she was wearing jeans, she'd be embarrassed and so would he, on account of then he'd have to tell her how even though he'd never even got a good look at her face before Thursday, he could've picked her out of a crowd anywhere.

''I probably ought to go up to bed. I'm thinking about checking on my apartment first thing tomorrow. It ought to be ready by now, don't you think?''

Jake didn't have to think. He reacted instinctively, easing the reins. ''Me, I'd give it a few more days, be sure they're all finished up and cleared out before I moved back in, but it's your call.''

He watched a frown pucker her feathery brown eyebrows, watched her lower lip get snagged by a gleaming white tooth. And then he sent his next signal. ''Did I tell you about the mares I picked up the other day? There's one I'd kind of like to show you, see what you think of her. She's got some age on her, but she's still got a lot of class. I thought we might ride down to the south boundary in the morning, sort of try out her paces. I can show you the prettiest little creek you ever saw, and you can tell me if you think she'll make a good ladies' mount. I've got in mind selling her to a dude ranch down near the Frio River canyon.''

His voice was easy, but there was a dark gleam in his eyes that made Priss think it was about time to say goodnight. If she was ever going to.

''Yes, well . . . that sounds real nice. Hmm. I'm not really an expert, you understand, but I guess I could—Jake, did you know your right eye is twitching?''

He shrugged. ''Tired, I guess.''

"You are, or your eyes are?"

"Both." Either he was closer or her own eyes were playing tricks. "Been reading too much fine print lately. Stuff gets smaller all the time. Priss—"

"You need to have your eyes examined."

He scowled. "Who, me? Hell, I'm only thirty-five."

"Yes, but—"

"Priss?"

It wasn't just her imagination. He *was* closer. So close she could see her own reflection in his eyes.

And then he kissed her. Again.

She could have pulled away. Probably should have if she knew what was good for her, but then, she'd never known that. All she knew at that moment was that she wanted his kiss more desperately than she had ever wanted anything in her life. The hard heat of Jake's body against hers. The soft feel of his hair under her fingers. The satiny texture of his skin, and his taste—

Oh, my, yes, the taste of him—sweet, smoky, intoxicating....

It was Priss who turned so that she was lying across his lap. It was Jake who found the small covered buttons that opened her dress on both shoulders. Before she quite knew what was happening, the soft, filmy fabric was caught on the tips of her breasts. And then he was kissing her there, his mouth leaving smoldering trails over the hills and valleys even as his hands explored the shape of her knees, her thighs, easing her full skirt up until the tops of her stockings were exposed.

She felt his breath catch at the sight of her bare skin, which, if she'd thought about it, would have surprised her, because skin was nothing unusual. Everybody had it. Most women showed more of it than she ever had, except in the swimming pool.

Although, come to think of it, as many bare male chests as she had seen in her lifetime, the sight of Jake's chest, with its scars and its wide patch of coarse curls and its flat brown nipples, had made her knees threaten to give way.

He was breathing hard, but then, so was she.

She knew he was aroused, because she could feel the hard ridge under her hip, straining against the front of his pants, and she wanted more than anything to touch him there, to explore him the way he was exploring her. To follow this aching, needy feeling wherever it led, and let tomorrow take care of tomorrow.

His fingertips had just edged under the lace of her panties when she heard him mutter something softly profane. Her thighs sort of fell apart of their own free will, and she was hot and wet and throbbing. She slipped her hand in between them, wriggling it down toward his belt— feeling the rippling muscles under her fingers as he reacted to her touch. It was the most thrilling thing she had ever experienced.

But it wasn't enough.

"Jake, could we—"

He caught her hand just as she felt the unnatural knob in a place that was usually perfectly flat. "Sweetheart, not here. Go easy, will you? I'm too old to pull a fool stunt like this." He groaned. His head fell back on the top of the sofa, and she stared at him, a little hurt, a little puzzled. Needing and wanting more than he was evidently willing to give her.

"Timing's off," he rasped. "Here comes Pete."

And there he came. They had barely scrambled halfway back to respectability when the old man waddled into the parlor bearing a tray filled with mismatched mugs, a can of evaporated milk and the crusty sugar bowl.

"You folks is mighty quiet in here. Want me to play ye some more music?"

A few hours later, her hair in rag rollers, a layer of revitalizing creme on her face and throat, and castor oil on the new calluses at the base of her fingers, Priss lay awake and wondered about a lot of things. Such as how a woman knew when she was in love with a man. Such as how to tell when a man was seriously interested in more than just sex. Such as whether sex alone would ever be enough in case he wasn't.

Staring into the darkness, her thoughts turned to a more practical matter, and she wondered if riding could really be all that difficult. The last time she'd been up on a horse, she'd been five years old. She had wanted a pony. Instead, her father had put her up on his own horse, a big bay gelding that stood some sixteen hands high and had small, mean eyes and big, yellow teeth. She'd been so far off the ground she'd been terrified and had begged to be taken off.

Her father had been so disgusted with her, he'd jerked her from the saddle, told her to grow up, and then stalked off and left her there in the paddock with the horse and the groom.

The groom, who smelled of rum, horse sweat and snuff, but was unfailingly kind, had set her outside the gate and told her to run home and ask Rosalie for some ice cream, but by then the damage had been done. She'd been scared of horses ever since. Not petrified scared—more like a healthy-respect scared.

On the other hand, once she'd conquered her fear of computers, she had learned to use one. She had learned to ski. She had learned when to plant what, when to prune what, and what would grow where. One year at summer camp, she had even learned to fly cast, although there wasn't a whole lot of call for fly fishermen around New Hope.

She could darn well learn to ride. Besides, she thought, punching her pillow and flopping restlessly onto her side, it was one more excuse to be with Jake.

But for someone who was so good at learning, she was still dumb as a stump when it came to learning to protect her heart. Going from Eddie to a man like Jake Spencer was like taking off her training wheels and climbing into the cockpit of an F-16.

So they rode. Jake could tell right off Priss was nervous. He tried to reassure her. And Priss tried to pretend it was a piece of cake, but he'd felt the tension in her when he'd taken her arm to steer her past the trough.

She admitted she hadn't ridden in a long time, and Jake thought, Yeah, like never.

But he didn't say anything. He owed her something to make up for her dancing lesson, and he'd already put the mare through her paces. She was steady as a rock, not likely to give trouble. Casually, so she wouldn't be embarrassed, he went over a few basics while he saddled up. "I'll be right there beside you, in case you get nervous or anything, all right?"

"I'm fine. You should've seen the first horse I ever rode, which was also the last one. He was big as an elephant, with mean-looking little eyes."

"Yeah? When was that?"

"I was five years old," she said, her quick glance daring him to make something out of it.

Jake shook his head. "Stirrups feel right? I can take 'em up some more."

"I'm fine," she said, a stiff, bright-eyed smile making him want to kiss her until she loosened up some.

Which probably wasn't a real good idea. "Her name is Rebecca's Baby Duckling."

"Goodness, that's a mouthful. Can I call her Becky?"

"Or Duck. Or Baby. It's your call."

She took a deep breath, beamed at him, and said in a voice that was only half an octave or so higher than usual, "Then, let's move 'em on out, Baby."

It was all Jake could do to keep from lifting her out of the saddle, holding her until some of the stiffness went out of her backbone and then laying her down in the nearest haystack and giving her another kind of riding lesson.

They set out at an easy pace on a southeast tack toward the creek, which was man-made, but old enough to be pretty, with trees and high grass, some rocks and a few wildflowers. He figured she'd like it, seeing as how she kept bringing up the lack of any bushes around the house.

He promised himself he wouldn't let things get out of hand again, and he meant it, too. She was a permanent kind of woman, and he was anything but.

On the other hand, he figured she owed him for that damned sausage. And his best and only suit. And his shirts. Not to mention all those nights when he'd come home from town after seeing her and hours later, he'd still be sitting out on the porch, nursing his solitary beer while he thought about ways of meeting her, ways of seducing her—ways he could satisfy the hunger she aroused in him.

As they rode, Jake pointed out the bungalows where Rico and Joe lived with their families. He showed her the new barn, the training pen, and the pasture where the rest of his new mares grazed peacefully, tails swishing away the flies.

"I've got a buyer interested already," he confided modestly. "Never hurts to rachet up a little bit of interest before a sale."

He told her about the roan stud, and talked a little bit about buying and selling horses, and she seemed genuinely interested, which led him to talk some more about his plans for improving the spread. "I'm not talking big, understand. Just quality. I don't need any more space than I have, but there's considerable work that still needs doing before I can sit back and relax."

"Everybody needs a goal," she said, and he thought about the short-term goal that had ended when he'd taken her into his home.

Leastwise, it was supposed to have ended. Funny thing, he couldn't seem to convince his body.

"Jake, did you ever think about getting married?"

He nearly swallowed his Adam's apple. "No, ma'am, I never did. Leastwise, not since I was old enough to know better." It was the truth. If he'd thought about it first, he never would've married Tammi.

"Oh."

He shot her a curious look. Had Faith been talking? He figured most folks around these parts knew he'd been married briefly, a long time ago—so long ago, it seemed like another lifetime.

"Well. I just thought I'd ask," she said, and then they rode on some more in silence while Jake sweated and wondered if he'd left his brains in his other hat.

They came to the creek and she stopped, shifting her weight and easing back on the reins just as he'd shown her. She wasn't exactly a natural, but she was a quick study, which sort of surprised him. A lot of things about the woman were beginning to surprise him.

"Jake, it's gorgeous!" she said, and he could tell she meant it.

Hell, it was only an irrigation ditch old man Holloman had dug forty or fifty years ago. Jake had never thought of it as gorgeous, but he had to admit it was a right pretty place. Dropping his reins, he went to lift her down, knowing she'd be pretty shaky after riding even this short distance. He was so proud of her he could bust. She'd hung in there. Hadn't asked any advice, either. She'd watched him like a hawk, and he'd been so caught up in his role as a silent teacher, he'd nearly forgot to enjoy the view of her butt rising over the cantle.

Which was probably just as well.

The trouble started when he lifted her down from the saddle. She more or less fell into his arms, and his arms just flat out refused to turn loose.

"Steady there," he said, and she laughed. The sound of that husky little chuckle wiped every scrap of common sense clean out of his head.

"Ah, Prissy, you don't make it easy on a guy, do you?"

"My legs are wobbly," she told him, as if that would explain it.

"They'll be stiff later on tonight," he said hoarsely.

That wasn't all that was going to be stiff. She had to know what was happening to him. It wasn't as if he could hide it. And, dammit, if she wasn't as turned on as he was, she was giving a pretty good imitation of it, hanging on to him the way she was, with her breathy little sighs and her sexy little wiggles.

One part of his brain whispered a warning.

Another part warned that if he let her go, he would regret it all the rest of his life.

As for Priss, it never even occurred to her to pretend. With Eddie it had been no problem. He'd wanted sex.

She'd wanted someone to go out with, to talk to, to dance with and flirt with. In the beginning, she'd wanted someone to fall in love with, but it hadn't taken long to realize that for her, it just wasn't going to happen.

With Jake, she wanted everything there was. She wanted what all those pregnant women running around in New Hope had had. And she wanted it with Jake. And she wanted it not just for now, but for always.

Nine

The two horses, Baby and Jake's gelding, Odd Job, grazed peacefully on the long, tender grass beside the creek. Insects droned in the summer heat, and a few small white wildflowers drooped on slender stems.

Priss was blind to it all. Her world began and ended in Jake's arms. She gazed up at him trustingly, a smile hovering at the corner of her mouth, because she felt too good to hold it in. It had been Jake who had invited her to go riding with him, after all. She hadn't pushed herself on him. It had been Jake who had insisted she come home with him in the first place. It hadn't been her idea. Which meant that no matter what he said, he wanted to be with her as much as she wanted to be with him.

He had kissed her three times already, and by now there was not a speck of doubt in her mind how she felt. At twenty-nine, there were some things a woman just knew.

She knew he wanted her. He must have known she was his for the asking, yet he hadn't taken advantage of her vulnerability. Which meant . . .

Which had to mean that no matter how much he protested otherwise, he was serious about her. She was no expert on men, but she did know most of them didn't really cotton to the idea of marriage. Women were the natural nesters. Men, on the other hand, were—

Well, men were whatever it was that men were, Lord love 'em.

For the first time in her life, Priss felt wise in ways that had nothing to do with schooling. Jake might be good at a lot of things, but it took a woman to tame a man, to make him want to settle down and start a family. That was the way it had always been, ever since Adam and Eve and the apple.

Leaning her face against the solid rock of his chest, she tightened her arms and tried to direct her mind toward a serious consideration of the future. His and hers. Theirs. Which wasn't easy when his heart was pounding so hard right under her ear.

One of his hands moved slowly up to caress the back of her neck, and then down again, curving over her hips, pressing her against him until she could feel every straining muscle of his body. She trembled. In danger of being swept away on a raging flood of passion, she clung to the only solid thing in the universe.

When Jake lowered her to the ground, she didn't utter a single word of protest. He removed his hat, sailed it over against a cottonwood tree, and knelt stiffly beside her. Without a second thought, she lifted her arms and he groaned and accepted her silent invitation.

"I reckon you need to rest a few minutes before we start back," he said, and she just smiled, feeling a rush of ancient womanly wisdom.

Priss knew what she needed, and it wasn't rest.

Jake brushed her hair back from her damp forehead, then carefully removed the pins she had just as carefully placed there that morning. He slipped them into his shirt pocket. "I've been wantin' to do that for years," he said, and she smiled again. Of course he didn't actually mean years. They'd only known each other for a few days. It was this feeling that had sprung up between them so quickly, almost as if they'd loved before, in another lifetime. Maybe they hadn't simply met one another that day in Faith's shop. Maybe they had *recognized* each other.

Priss's mind was awash with compelling new ideas. Her body was awash with even more compelling feelings. Jake was toying with a few strands of hair, winding them around his finger, smoothing them with his thumb. "Honey, you need to understand something before we go any further. I'm not sure just how to say it . . ."

He didn't have to say it. She *knew*.

"The thing is, there's a lot of work to do around a place like this. I made a promise to myself a long time ago, after—well, let's just say I haven't made many promises over the years, but those I do make, I'm obliged to keep."

"Jake, you don't have to explain anything, I understand," she murmured. They were two of a kind. She didn't make promises lightly, either. It was a good thing she'd shown him how willing she was to work, how quickly she could learn once she set her mind to it. "I feel the same way."

He sort of frowned at that, and she thought he might not be convinced yet, but that was no problem. She had the rest of her life to convince him that when something was meant to be, why, then, it was purely meant to be.

She laid her palm on the side of his neck and felt the pulse pounding there. With her newfound confidence and daring, she lifted her head and bit him gently on the chin, then touched the wound with her tongue.

Jake shuddered violently, his eyes tightly shut. "Take it easy, sweetheart," he growled.

Sweetheart. Oh, how she loved the sound of that word.

He trailed a fingertip down her throat to the opening of her white silk shirt. Her heart skipped a beat and then doubled its rhythm.

"Sunup to sundown," he muttered, his voice a hoarse rasp against the lazy, summer-afternoon chorus of insects. "Not much time to spare in between. Sometimes I don't even get to bed until it's near about time to get up again. It's a hard enough life for a single man. For a—"

"Shh. I told you, I understand." She kissed the palm of his hand as he caressed her cheek, and he shook his head and sighed.

As cooler air brushed over the heated skin of her breasts, Priss felt desperately vulnerable and at the same time, almost feverishly joyful. "But if you're all that busy, I'd hate to think I was keeping you from something important," she teased.

He lowered his head and she could feel his breath hot on her throat. On her breast. He had unbuttoned her shirt and laid it open, and she knew that if he hadn't, she would have torn it open. She wanted to feel his hands on her body—his lips on her body.

His full weight on her body.

He said something about long-term plans, but she didn't listen because at the moment she was more interested in what he was doing to her than in what he was saying to her.

Then, with a deep, urgent groan, he took her mouth with a sexual urgency that robbed her of the last fleeting thought. She strained against him, holding him to her with both arms as he slid his body over hers and ground his hips against her aching pelvis. He was blatantly aroused. Priss felt a glimmer of fear that was gone almost as swiftly as it had arisen.

His belt buckle cut into her belly, and she wanted to tell him to take it off—to take everything off, only he was still kissing her and she didn't ever want him to stop.

When one of his hands inched its way under her back, she lifted one shoulder to allow him access to her bra hook and made up her mind to call that little French place at the Galleria and order a dozen front-hooked bras to be delivered immediately.

He murmured something that sounded like "Perfect" and "Made for me," and her breast swelled to meet his questing lips.

"I know," she whispered.

Of course they were made for each other. His subconscious mind knew it, even if his conscious mind would never in a million years admit it. That was just one of the differences between men and woman. One of the many lovely differences . . .

Priss's hands moved down over his hips, savoring the feel of his taut buttocks. He shuddered. His mouth on her breast grew momentarily still, and then he ground his lower body against hers, and she wondered how long it could be before he took off all his clothes, and hers, too, and did what they both wanted until neither of them could speak a coherent sentence.

Priss knew about desire. She might not be terribly experienced, but she knew how it felt, and besides, she had read articles.

Jake paused in the middle of unzipping her jeans to say something about understanding how it was, and she cried impatiently, "Yes! Jake, please hurry, can you?"

Mercy, was that Priss Barrington making those demands? She didn't even recognize herself!

He fumbled with the hook of the concho belt she had paid a small fortune for, and she wanted to cry, *Cut it off! Tear it loose! Hurry, hurry, before I melt!*

Frantically, she tugged at his shirttail. Lifting his body for one brief moment, Jake yanked it free, unclipped his belt, and tore two buttons off his shirt. Priss wondered fleetingly if she should find them and save them to sew back on for him, but then she stopped thinking again.

Oh, my. He was beautiful. She told him so, and he grinned, but he didn't look all that amused. In fact, he looked more like he was in pain.

She reached up and slipped his shirt off his shoulders. While he supported his weight on first one arm and then the other, she pulled it free and tossed it aside. Seeing his scars again, she winced. They weren't pretty, but they were a part of him, so she kissed them, wishing she could have been there at the time to kiss away the hurt, the way Rosalie used to kiss away hers.

Kissing the scars scattered over his chest and shoulder led to kissing the small, flat brown nipples, savoring the clean, salty taste of his skin. When he shuddered and swore softly under his breath, pushing his male breast against her mouth, Priss felt as if she were about to explode with the sheer joy of love.

He lifted his head and gazed down at her, and she thought, How harsh he looks, with his cheekbones all flushed and angular. Her Jake. Her man. She had seen him in a teasing mood. She had seen him when he was angry, when he was concerned. Now she was seeing him honed to a sharp edge of desire.

"Priss—honey, you do know how I feel, don't you? I explained . . ."

She nodded, so full of love and happiness she couldn't have spoken if she tried. She knew how he felt. She felt the same way. They were in love, and he had warned her that from now on, life wouldn't be at all the way it used to be when she lived in her father's house, with servants and nothing more to do than shop and get her legs waxed and her hair and nails done on schedule.

She had known he was kind. In spite of his shabby clothes, he had a kind of bred-in-the-bone integrity that she recognized almost from the first. "I know, darling, I feel the same way. I'm a big girl now. I know what's—" She broke off, inhaling with a long, shuddery gasp. "Ahhh, would you do that to me again? It makes me feel all lazy and bubbly and warm, like hot molasses . . ."

And so he did it to her again, and then he lifted her hips and slid her jeans down her legs, and the hot molasses flowed thicker and swifter until she was drowning in the dark, sweet joy of it all.

Jake had protection, but he'd been carrying it around in his wallet for so long that he couldn't guarantee it wouldn't come apart under the strain. So he asked her point-blank, "Priss, are you on the pill?"

She didn't think he meant vitamins, and she wasn't taking anything else, so she shook her head.

"Is it a safe time of the month for you? I mean, I can protect you, but a little backup might not be a bad thing."

It took a few moments for her to realize what he'd been talking about, and because he seemed so concerned he might stop if she told him she was right in the middle of her cycle, which she'd been keeping track of with a thermometer even before she'd gone to the clinic—she lied. There wasn't that big a chance, anyway. And besides, they'd be getting married as soon as he felt he could spare the time from all he had to do around here.

"I'm safe," she said, and was a little shocked at the feeling of guilt that came over her. Except for the polite little white lies she told on occasion to spare someone's feelings, she was truthful by nature. But then, wasn't this one of those occasions?

And then, all feelings of guilt were swallowed up by a hoard of other feelings.

Jake counted slowly to ten. He could've counted to ten thousand and it wouldn't have helped. He'd sworn he wouldn't rush things, because he might not get another chance. Maybe they could come to some sort of an understanding, but in case they couldn't—in case this was the one and only time in his life he could live out a fantasy— he was determined to make it as good for her as he possibly could. So that at least she would remember him once she was back in that plush apartment of hers, and tooling around town in her vintage Caddy convertible.

With some other guy.

Some other guy who would take her to some swank club and feed her all kinds of fancy food, and dance with her and drink wine with her, and then go home with her and make love to her and wake up the next morning in her fancy bed on her fancy flowered sheets with the scent of her perfume—

"Jake?"

He swallowed hard. "Yeah. Priss—honey, are you sure you're sure?"

"I'm sure," she said simply. "But if you've changed your mind . . ."

He laughed, but there was little amusement in the sound. With trembling fingers, he finished undressing them both, then lowered himself into the cradle of her thighs. One part of him wanted to stand over her and gaze down on her sundappled body with its full, firm breasts, the sweeping incurve of her waist and the slight swell of her belly. His first glimpse of the thatch of dark gold curls between her womanly thighs nearly brought tears to his eyes. She was so perfect. And *real*—not like one of those skinny fashion models.

She deserved to be pleasured, and if he couldn't offer her anything else, he could give her that.

Slowly, carefully, Jake brought her to the peak of desire, using every skill at his command. He loved her with his hands, with his lips, with his tongue. By the time he eased his painfully aroused shaft into her threshold, he was half out of his mind.

By the time he realized she was a virgin, it was too late.

Unable to hold back, he thrust wildly, again and again. Finally he shuddered and collapsed, allowing his head to fall onto her shoulder while he struggled to recover from what had been the single most powerful experience of his life.

"Why didn't you tell me?" he whispered harshly when he could once more command his wits.

Priss didn't pretend not to know what he was talking about. He had to have heard her gasp—she'd read somewhere that men could always tell, but then, she'd also read that they couldn't, and anyway, what difference did it make? "I didn't think it mattered."

Rolling off her, Jake lay face down, his head resting on his crossed arms. He didn't speak, and Priss reached down and tugged a shirt—his, as it happened—over her naked body. Nearby, a frog croaked. A flock of crows landed noisily in the cottonwood and took off again, loudly protesting the intrusion. She didn't hear any of it.

Watching for some clue as to what was wrong, she studied the long form stretched out beside her in the grass. From the waist up, he was brown. And smooth, except for those little tufts of hair under his arms and the thicket she knew was right in the middle of his chest. From the waist down, he was white and hairy. She thought it was a remarkably fine combination. "Jake? Is something wrong?" She knew she probably hadn't done it right, but surely he understood that with a little practice, she'd do better. She knew the mechanics of it now. With a little practice she would master the art.

He turned onto his side and glared at her. "Damn right there's something wrong. You lied to me!"

Bolting upright, she glared right back. "I did n— Well, maybe I did, but it wasn't a big lie."

And anyway, how did he know for sure? Without one of those little kits, even she couldn't know for sure that she was fertile, and even if she was, it was a longshot. And anyhow, he'd worn one of those thingies, hadn't he?

"What do you mean, not a big lie? Honey, if you've hung on to your virginity this long, losing it is no small deal. What I want to know is why? What the devil did you hope to gain?"

So much for her newfound womanly wisdom. Priss had mistaken what had upset him, but she didn't mistake the "honey" for an endearment. Not this time. Not spoken in that scathing tone of voice. "I don't think that's any of your business. And anyway, you can't be sure I was a virgin. I read this article once that said that except in a few cases, men couldn't—"

"Oh, yeah? Well, *this* man can! And just in case you've got some harebrained notion of cashing in on it, you can forget it, because like I told you right up front, I'm not in the market for any long-term deals.''

"Fine. Good. Because I'm not, either, and even if I were, I wouldn't—I w-wouldn't—"

Scrambling onto her hands and knees, Priss gathered her scattered clothing and started putting it on, not daring to look at Jake. Hoping he wasn't looking at her. Hoping he had taken a flying leap into that damned creek, which was only a few feet deep but would serve the purpose.

Oh, this is all wrong! This isn't the way it was supposed to happen!

After cramming her bare feet into her boots and stuffing her socks under her belt, she stomped over to where the two horses were grazing. "Come here, horse," she snarled, hoping the blasted thing knew more about this riding business than she did. She snatched up the reins and tried to remember which side she was supposed to mount from. Lefty, loosey, righty, tighty.

No, that was faucets.

Evidently, she did it the right way, because Babe didn't seem to object. Wiggling her bottom back and forth, she clucked the patient mare into a leisurely stroll.

Jake watched her go. They were probably both going to wind up covered with chigger bites, but that was the least of his problems.

And hers. Leastwise, if she thought that just because she'd given up her virginity, he was bound to marry her.

Given it up? Hell, she'd all but forced it on him!

She was twenty-nine years old. No woman kept it that long anymore. Not unless she was some kind of a nut case.

Which Priss was, only not that kind of a nut case. Actually, as nuts went, she was a pretty nice one. He had to admit he'd gotten a kick out of the way she'd thrown her-

self into everything she'd tackled, from cooking to washing to ironing—even if she had loused it up.

But dammit, sex was something else again, especially
where a woman's virginity was concerned. She couldn't
have thought he would marry her, because he'd made that
plain right from the first. They had come together because they both wanted it, pure and simple. And because
they were both free. And there wasn't a single reason under the sun why they shouldn't.

Slowly, Jake got dressed, wondering how he'd have felt
if one of the hands had ridden out to see what all the
ruckus was about, with crows cutting up at having their
watering hole taken over.

He whistled up Odd Job, wishing he'd had the good
sense to ride the roan stud. Before he saw Priss again, he
had some serious thinking to do, and he always thought
better after a good hard workout.

All the way back to the house, Priss went over in her
mind the words that had been said. Not what had been
done, because she would never forget that, but it was what
had been said she needed to remember now. Somewhere
buried in the few words they'd spoken, there had to be a
clue.

Pete had returned from wherever he'd gone that morning. He greeted her from the kitchen door when she tried
to sneak past and go upstairs. "Shoulda wore a hat. Ladies' skin is delicate." He was drying a cast-iron frying pan
on a towel that looked less than pristine.

"I never wear hats," she said, trying to dredge up a
smile for the old man who had treated her like a cross between a favorite niece and an apprentice housekeeper.

"Might ought to. Keeps the grass out'n yer hair."

"I've got to go—to go upstairs and pack," she said quickly.

Pete came out into the hall and watched her as she clumped up the bare painted steps. "Look like you've been rode—"

Priss could feel herself blushing. She said without turning around, "I know, I know. Like I've been rode hard and put away wet."

And then she blushed even harder.

Ten

Shutting the bedroom door behind her, Priss closed her eyes and leaned against the cool painted surface. For one long moment she allowed herself to think about what had happened. She'd always wondered what it would be like. What woman in her circumstances wouldn't? She had been tempted once or twice, but never tempted quite enough to forget all her parents' strictures.

So now it had finally happened. Now she knew. It had been—

She dismissed the word *fate*, but the word *inevitable* occurred to her. Wildly exciting, of course. Also uncomfortable. Maybe even embarrassing, if she'd had time to think about it. All in all, it had been . . . almost wonderful, she decided. Until Jake had said those awful things, and she'd said things right back at him.

It occurred to her that the last time she'd climbed this far out on a limb, she had fallen and broken her arm.

This time, she was afraid it might be more than an arm that had been broken. But then, if there was one thing she was good at—had learned to be good at over a lot of years—it was hiding her feelings and going on as if nothing had happened.

Dragging out her luggage, Priss plopped it on the bed, then began emptying drawers and dragging things out of the chiffonier. It was amazing how deeply she had settled in after no more than a few days. No wonder Jake thought she was trying to squeeze herself a place in his life.

Wheeling around, she marched to the head of the stairs and yelled downstairs. "Pete, can you drive me to town this afternoon?"

The old man emerged from the kitchen. He was still drying the frying pan. Priss suspected he'd been watching television and used the frying pan and towel so that he'd look busy in case anyone came in. "Can't Jake drive you in?"

"He's busy. He said so." He'd said that and a whole lot more.

A hard lump formed in her throat. Ignoring it, she went back to her packing. She thought about calling the super out at Willow Creek Arms to be sure her apartment was ready for occupancy and decided against it. No matter what anyone said, she was moving in. If he tried to stall her again, why then, she would just use it as a lever to break her lease and find herself a house. Something small. With a yard big enough for a garden and maybe some play equipment. Something near a school.

Phooey on Jake Spencer. Who needed him?

Booted feet ringing out on the bare painted floor, she marched back and forth between chiffonier and bed until all her bags were packed. Just as she snapped the last one shut, she heard Jake come in and head up the stairs. There was no mistaking that purposeful tread.

Priss didn't want to talk to him. Not now. Probably not ever. He could take his blasted long-term deals and go straight to blue blazes, because she wouldn't marry him now if he went down on bended knee and begged her.

If he could even bend one. Having seen the scars on his body, including one on his left leg where the bone had evidently been badly broken, she wondered that he got around as well as he did.

Not that he hadn't managed beautifully down beside the creek . . .

He was coming upstairs. Well, damn.

Acting on impulse, Priss dashed across the hall to the bathroom and slammed the door behind her.

Jake's firm, gritty footsteps paused outside the bathroom door. "Pricilla? We need to talk."

She turned the old-fashioned door latch and then opened both faucets in the tub.

"Priss? Open the door. Please?"

The heavy lump in her throat slipped down into her chest, where it began to ache. "I'm busy," she growled. For good measure, she flushed the commode.

"Dammit, woman, we need to talk!"

"Then talk." She sniffled and wiped an arm across her eyes. She wouldn't cry, she *would not*. What was done was done, and crying wasn't going to change anything.

For one split second she thought he was going to break in the door. She watched the old porcelain knob twist and rattle. It was probably a hundred years old, and about as secure as a paperclip.

"Judas priest," she heard him mutter, and then she heard him stomp off down the hallway. Burying her face in her hands, she sat down on the commode and bawled, which eased the ache in her chest, but didn't do much for her heart.

She couldn't even blame Jake, not really. Mostly it was her own fault. Every time he kissed her, she kissed him right back. He had to know how she felt—she hadn't even tried to hide it, she'd been so sure he felt the same way.

Well, starting right now, that was going to change. If she could love a man, she could darn well *un*love him.

He had his long-term plans? So did she, and they didn't include any busted-up ex-rodeo cowboy who called every woman he met "honey" and "sugar" and "darling."

And sweetheart. Oh, she'd really fallen for that one.

Right now he was probably waiting at the bottom of the stairs to get her signature on a release form, absolving him of any responsibility for deflowering her.

Deflowering. What a silly, stupid term. Priss didn't know where it had come from—Rosalie, probably. She was pretty sure it hadn't come from *Cosmopolitan*.

Anyway, at her age, virginity was a joke. Jake hadn't taken anything from her. She had given it of her own free will, but he could roast on a spit in hell before she would let him deflower her again.

He wasn't waiting at the bottom of the steps, after all. By the time Priss had lugged all her cases down to the front door, there was still no sign of him. Uncertain whether to be relieved or disappointed, she went through the kitchen and poked her head in the office. "Pete? I'm ready. If you'll pull your truck around front, I'll lug this stuff out-side."

The old man stalked past her and grabbed up the heaviest suitcase. "Take that there tinsiest one, I'll fetch the rest. Jake gimme the keys to his truck so them fancy bags o' yourn wouldn't git ruint slippey-slidin' around in the back o' my ole rust bucket."

* * *

Three days later, on Thursday, Rosalie came back from Dallas, full of snapshots, pickled okra and thank-you notes from her family. She wasted no time in fussing over the shadows under Priss's eyes and the wan look on her face. "You ain't been eatin' right."

Priss assured her it was merely the remnants of a bug she'd picked up at the hospital the last time she'd gone out to read to the children.

Six days after that, when the super chased her out of the entrance shrubbery where she'd been planting a simple border of dusty miller, Priss made up her mind to look for a small house with a moderate price tag and a generous-size yard.

Fortunately, her car was back from the shop, as good as new. She drove in to New Hope General three times in a single week to read to the children, although sometimes they wanted to talk, so she just listened to them while they tried to outdo each other telling tall tales. She even told a few of her own, which they all seemed to enjoy.

Rosalie, fresh from managing the lives of her great-nieces and nephews like a five-star general, was still in her fussing mode. Priss wasn't getting enough sleep. She wasn't eating enough to keep a fly alive. She was drooping like a rainy Monday. At breakfast on Friday morning, just two weeks after she'd met Jake, Priss claimed she wasn't hungry, and the elderly woman accused her of moping over what she called that shameful baby notion.

"Miss Agnes had the right of it. If your daddy was alive today, he'd whomp some sense into your head! Now you set down there and eat your breakfast and quit talkin' all that crazy business 'bout babies!"

Priss sat. She even ate a few bites of waffle, but it reminded her of the awful mess she had made of cooking a meal for Jake, which reminded her of too many other things, so she crumpled her napkin over her plate and escaped the minute Rosalie went back to watching "The Morning Show" and shelling peas.

The baby notion. There were two things Priss regretted. One was getting mixed up with Jake Spencer in the first place. But as long as she had, her second regret was not discussing with him, in a calm and rational way, the possibility of his fathering her baby and then letting her raise it on her own. That would have been better than nothing.

In fact, it would've been the perfect solution. As for marriage, they really didn't have all that much in common, except for that infernal itch they had scratched in a weak moment.

Oh, for a little while she had thought they were destined to be together. She'd thought about what fun they could have, making a real home out of that awful old house. For a little while she'd been sure she sensed a secret well of loneliness buried deep inside the man, and she'd responded to it instinctively.

She'd been wrong, of course. Jake wasn't lonely. He was too mule-headed ever to allow himself to need anyone except maybe Pete, and even that, she suspected, was because Pete needed to be needed.

If he ever married anyone, it wouldn't be a woman who couldn't cook, couldn't do his laundry without shrinking his pants and burning holes in his shirts, who couldn't even ride a horse without flopping around in the saddle like a fifty-pound sack of meal.

All the same, she wished she had asked him right up-front about the baby thing. If he ever found out—not that she was one hundred percent certain she was pregnant—but if she was, and if Jake ever did find out, he'd raise a ruckus that would be heard all the way to Montana.

Well. Time would tell. In the meantime, just in case, she made another appointment at the sperm bank, and this time she was careful to make it on Miss Agnes's day off.

It was one of the hottest Julys on record. Priss went to Dallas, determined to make some serious changes in her life. She spent an entire afternoon at the Galleria, trying on neat little classics. She toyed with the idea of having her hair cut and done in one of those sleek, understated styles her mother had always favored. "In New Hope, Pricilla Joan, there are girls who wear big hair and girls who amount to something," her mother had told her more than once.

At twenty-nine, Priss finally knew *who she was,* and liked that person just fine, thank you.

So she gave up on the classics and the new hair style and bought a handsome coral-and-turquoise squash blossom necklace instead. And a darling Guatemalan embroidered smock, just in case. And a precious pink straw hat covered with big silk cabbage roses for one of the little girls who was undergoing chemotherapy.

It was two weeks later that she saw Jake again. Exactly six weeks past the day they had made love by the creek and she had packed her bags and left the Bar Nothing forever. In the back of her mind, she'd always known that sooner or later she would see him again. Sooner or later, everyone saw everyone in New Hope. It was that kind of a town.

But of all the days for it to happen. Fate really had it in for her. She had just found out she was one hundred percent certain, and had raced down to the shop to tell Faith and compare a few notes on the early stages of pregnancy when there he came, striding through the door with that shoulder-swinging, hip-switching walk of his, like John

Wayne in one of those old movies, accompanied by the tiny jingle of the bell over the door.

Priss's heart did a quiet little flipflop while she waited for him to greet Faith, who was finishing up with a couple of customers. She watched as he worked his way back to where she stood, trying desperately to look nonchalant.

When he was halfway between the books and the Raggedy Ann and Andy dolls, she braced herself to greet him as she would any other casual acquaintance, never mind that he was the first—and so far, the only—man she had ever made love to.

The only man she had ever fallen in love with enough to think about marriage, although she was working hard at getting over that.

The jingle of the bell announced that another man had entered the shop. Priss ignored him as she tried not to stare at Jake. Had she thought he was handsome? He wasn't. Not really. He looked, she thought, her heart aching fit to bust, like a Clint Black who'd been rode hard and put away wet, only taller. Those same familiar faded jeans, the worn boots—that same weathered face with the sharp cheekbones, slashing black eyebrows and steely gray eyes.

It all came rushing back, everything she had tried so hard to forget. The way he had nearly broken his neck trying to catch her when she tripped over his feet right here in the Baby Boutique that first day. The way he'd gone racing out to the apartments to help her the minute he heard about the fire.

She thought of how he had tried to spare her feelings after their first disastrous meal together, and how sweet and stern he had looked concentrating on not trampling her feet when she'd been teaching him how to dance... although she rather thought he wasn't quite as inexperienced as he pretended to be.

Oh, he cared for her, all right, she knew he did. Only not enough.

Jake dodged past a woman in a maternity smock and briefly Priss considered dashing into the stockroom and out the back door. As busy as the shop was today, she wasn't going to get to share her big news with Faith anyway.

But then Faith spotted the man who had entered the store right behind Jake and said, "Mitch? Mitch McCord, I haven't seen you in ages!" As soon as she spoke, Jake swung around, said something about a small world and stuck out his hand, and the two men shook hands and slapped each other on the back a few times.

Priss stood where she was, feeling left out, which wasn't a particularly new feeling. She didn't know Mitch McCord from Adam, but she resented his stealing Jake's attention, even if she hadn't wanted to see Jake, herself.

Faith took care of the introductions. "Priss, meet Mitch McCord. Mitch, this is Priss Barrington. Mitch is rumored to have stolen almost as many hearts in his high school days as Jake here. You remember Jake, don't you, Priss? You two met right here in my store on the Fourth of July?"

"The first," they both said together.

Then Jake said, "Yeah, she remembers. Mitch, good to see you. Priss, you want to ride out to the park with me?"

Before Priss could come up with an excuse or an answer, Faith turned to Mitch. "What on earth are you doing shopping in a baby store? Don't tell me you're thinking about getting married and starting a family? You and Jake here are the last of New Hope's professional bachelors—although I guess, strictly speaking, Jake can't be called a bachelor anymore."

He couldn't? The old familiar lump settled in Priss's chest, and she wondered what could have changed in the past six weeks.

Surely he wasn't married. There hadn't been any mention of a wedding in the paper lately. Even if he'd married somewhere else, the local paper would have printed a few lines.

Then Mitch spoke. "Look, I really need some help, Faith. Can you fix me up with whatever it takes to look after a baby?"

"What baby? How old is it? Boy or girl? And for how long are you taking care of it? Mitch shopping for a baby isn't exactly the same as shopping for a new set of tires."

Jake pursed his lips thoughtfully. "It's a lot more expensive, for one thing."

Mitch McCord raked a hand through his hair. "All I know is that somebody left a baby—in a basket—on my doorstep—with a note saying to take care of my baby. *My* baby! Can you beat that?"

Jake looked as if he were struggling to hold back a grin, which Priss considered downright insensitive since Mitch was obviously a friend of his, and the poor man seemed distraught.

"Is it yours?" Faith asked.

Mitch shrugged. "Could be. Might be. Yeah, I guess so. At least that's what the note said."

"In that case, we'd better start putting together a layette."

"A what?"

"Chickens finally coming home to roost, huh?" Jake said, his grin finally breaking through.

Mitch glowered at him. "Just wait. Your turn'll come one of these day, and then we'll see who has the last laugh.

Faith, what about one of those car basket gadgets? And maybe a book of instructions?''

Priss handed over the book she'd been leafing through. "I guess it's too late for this, huh?"

"Prenatal Nutrition? Yeah, I guess. Little beauty looks healthy enough to me."

"You've got a daughter," Jake said, and Priss thought, amazed, that he sounded almost envious. "Better take one of these, then." He selected a soft, fuzzy baby seal and set it on the counter.

"And these," Priss said, not to be outdone. Her contribution was three boxes of disposable diapers.

"How old is she?" Faith, always practical, was holding up a tiny knit romper suit of blue-and-yellow striped cotton with an orange sailboat on the bib.

"How old?" A flash of panic appeared in Mitch's eyes, which Jake seemed to find amusing and Priss found touching.

"Jake, stop teasing," Priss said. "Mitch—can she sit up alone? Does she say anything? Ma-ma? Da-da?"

"Oh, I don't know. Mostly, she just drools and wets her diapers. I left her with Jenny next door while I made a supply run."

Priss, busy selecting clothes for Mitch's baby girl, but with her own unborn child in mind, said absently, "Jenny Stevens? I know her. We met at the engagement party Faith gave Mike and Michelle last February. Jenny said she had some mulberry seedlings I could have, but the super wouldn't let me plant them at the apartment. You remember meeting Jenny at the engagement party, don't you, Faith?"

Glass scattered everywhere as Faith dropped a lamp in the shape of a blue dinosaur. She just stood there, a stricken look on her face. After a startled moment of surprise, Mitch picked up a piece of broken lamp. Jake took Faith by the arm and led her over to the wicker settee, telling her to sit tight while he cleaned up the broken glass. Priss headed for the back room after a broom and dustpan, and Faith sat, her face as red as a West Texas sunset.

It didn't take more than a few minutes to restore order, and by then, Faith seemed to have recovered from whatever ailed her. Priss thought it might have something to do with Faith's being pregnant. "That reminds me," Priss said in a surprised tone. "The Russo wedding is set for November—the same month your baby is due, Faith. Two blessed events in one month, isn't that wonderful?"

Faith paled, then hurried out of her chair and practically ran toward the back room. "If you'll excuse me for just a moment. Mitch, gather up everything and I'll be right back to ring it up."

Jake picked up Priss's hand and laced his fingers through hers. "Ready to shove off?" he said, as if they had parted only yesterday on the best of terms.

Nothing had changed. His touch still set off fireworks.

She tried and failed to extract her fingers from his deceptively gentle grip. "Maybe I'd better stay," she murmured. "Faith might need me."

Faith came back into the room and waved off the idea. "Beth's coming in at one. Go ahead, I'll talk to you in a few days."

"You heard the lady," Jake said. He was smiling, but his eyes had that stainless-steel look she had learned to dread. "See you around town, McCord. Good luck with little whatshername."

Outside, the heat slammed up from the sidewalk. There wasn't a hint of cloud in the sky. "Your friend could probably have used some moral support," Priss said, try-

ing to sound cross, succeeding only in sounding breathless. She tugged at her hand, and he released it.

"Maybe I'm not in a supportive mood."

"In that case, why don't you go back out to your horse
farm? You don't need to see me to my car."

"I didn't plan to. I told you we needed to talk."

"If you'd had anything to say, you could have said it
before I left."

"You were barricaded in the bathroom, remember?"

Barricaded was the right word for it. And dammit, it
was just as bad as ever. One look from those clear, cool
eyes of his and Priss sizzled right down to her toes. One
word and she started scrambling around in her mind, trying to remember all the reasons why she didn't really love
him.

One touch and it all came back to her. Instant recall. His
body—the scars. The thicket of black hair on his chest,
and the other one at his groin, not to mention the fasci-
nating expanse of tautly muscled flesh in between.

And the way his body made her body feel . . .

His truck was parked outside the boutique in the blaz-
ing sun. Her car was parked down the street behind the
bank, in what little shade there was to be found down-
town in the middle of the day in August. Her personal
banker always saved her a parking place in the shade on
Fridays. It was just one of those little courtesies that went
along with being *who she was*.

They sat in Jake's truck with the engine running and the
air conditioner going full-blast. It was several minutes before either of them spoke a word.

Priss could have waited all day. She hadn't the least idea
what he wanted to talk about, but she suspected it was
something she'd just as soon not hear. If he'd had any-

thing important to say to her, he would have said it that day down by the creek.

"Town's got more wagging tongues than a kennelful of hounds," he muttered, leaning back against the corner of the metallic-gray cab.

"Is that what you wanted to talk about? Miss Agnes, Miss Minny and Miss Ethel's latest bulletins?"

"You got that right. I reckon Miss Agnes started it, seein' as how she works there, but now the whole town's chewing on it. Rico's wife came home from taking her kid to the dentist and said she heard you'd gone and got yourself a baby from the sperm bank."

As a mere receptionist, Miss Agnes wasn't privy to all that went on at the sperm bank. Even so, Priss should have known what would happen. A body couldn't change brands of toothpaste without the whole town's being in on it, even if they got the brand names mixed up.

Priss had always assumed that Jake would find out someday, only it was too soon. Too close to what had happened between them, and besides, she wasn't nearly as immune to him as she'd hoped. These things took time.

"So?" It was the best she could come up with. It wasn't much, but then, she'd always fallen back on attitude in an emergency.

"So." That single, tight-lipped word tipped her off to the fact that he was mad as hornets and trying hard to hang on to his temper.

Priss was tempted to repeat it again, but didn't quite dare. They were already beginning to sound like a couple of school kids starting a shoving match.

With one sweep of his hand, Jake knocked his hat back into the jump seat. Glaring at her, he said, "So why the devil didn't you let me give you a baby if you wanted one all that much?"

Eleven

Jake, still talking about talking, headed out toward the park, stopping off at Little Joe's to buy four chili dogs, a beer and half a pint of milk. The milk was for Priss. For some reason she'd ordered milk, rather than a diet cola.

Priss wanted to tell him she was in no mood for a picnic, much less any lectures, but the odor of food reminded her that she had skipped breakfast again, and last night's dinner had consisted of a stack of Oreo cookies spread with peanut butter.

She was debating the size of the lie she could get away with when he made a U-turn in the middle of Burrus Boulevard and headed out of town at a high rate of speed. "What are you doing?" she demanded.

"I wish to hell I knew," he muttered.

It's the heat, Priss thought. Either that or he was undergoing an early midlife crisis. Was that only a male thing? Because it occurred to her that she might be having one, too.

Not until they passed Buck's Texaco and Barbecue did she know for certain where they were headed. And then she wondered why.

"Is Pete all right?" It was the first thing that popped into her mind—that Pete might be sick and Jake needed someone to look after him, and he'd heard about her being a volunteer at the hospital. "Because if he's sick, I'm real good with children, but I'm not so sure about adults."

The look he gave her defied description. It wasn't the first time he'd looked at her that way. "Pete's fine. He's visiting up Denton way. He'll be back sometime tomorrow."

A few miles down the road she said, "You mentioned talking?"

"Yeah."

Half a mile later she added, "So?"

"I reckon Faith told you I'm a bastard."

Priss's mouth fell open. "She did no such thing! Faith thinks you're real nice."

Jake began to chuckle, and although she hadn't a clue as to what he found amusing, Priss thought it was just about the most satisfying sound she'd ever heard. He said, "I don't go around pulling little girls' pigtails anymore, if that's what you mean by nice. What I mean is, my old man never got around to marrying my mama. Didn't even come close."

His left arm was resting on the open window, his right one on the steering wheel. Priss just had to touch something, because at heart, she was a hands-on kind of person. Since his hands were either occupied or out of reach, she settled for his thigh. "Oh, Jake, I'm so sorry," she said, squeezing hard. "Fathers can come in real handy, but to tell you the truth, they're not always what they're cracked up to be. Mine wanted a son. Instead, he only got me, and Mama said, no way would she go thought that miserable business again. Having a baby, I mean. And being pregnant. I think she was sick a lot, and Daddy never did have much patience with sickness."

Somehow, without quite knowing how it came about, Priss was telling him all about the gardener who had nurtured her interest in plants, and Miss Agnes, who had tattled on her the time she snuck into the Methodist Vacation Bible School when everybody in town knew Barringtons had always been Presbyterians, and she'd got another good talking to about *who she was* and *her kind of people*, and other italic things.

Which led to Jake's telling her about his brief marriage, and how he'd been in debt from the time he was fifteen years old and had dropped out of school to look after his mama, and about the running account he had with a florist for the flowers he put on her grave every week. "She always liked roses a lot. There was one kind, sort of pink and yellow—she was hog-wild over those."

"Peace," Priss told him, and he sent her a perplexed look but said Peace right back at her.

"It's the name of the rose. I saw some once at the botanical gardens in Dallas. Did she ever go there? It's out on Garland Road."

"I don't know," he said simply, and from the hollow sound of his voice, she suspected he was thinking about all the other things he would never know about his mother, and the things he'd never been able to do for her and wished now that he had. Priss had felt that way, herself, since her parents died, and she hadn't even been all that close to them.

"It's always that way when it's too late, isn't it? I used to try so hard to be pale and slender and beautiful," she said to make him feel better. "For my mama," she explained when he asked her what the devil she was talking about. "All Mama's people were good-looking. I used to think everybody in Virginia must be beautiful, to hear Mama talk about her cousins and all, but I took after Daddy's side of the family, and whatever else he was, nobody ever called him good-looking."

Jake gripped the steering wheel so hard his hands hurt. He was furious with her parents for not appreciating what they had, and furious with Priss for caring too much.

It struck him that in some ways, they weren't all that different. Both of them were misfits, although he'd always preferred to think of himself as a loner.

The first thing Priss noticed when they turned off the main road was that the Bar Nothing sign had been given a new coat of paint. Dark green on pale yellow, with a barred zero between the two words. She still thought the name was kind of silly, but the sign looked neat and attractive.

"You've resurfaced the driveway," she exclaimed.

They were rattling toward the house at a pretty good clip—fast enough to send small chunks of gravel pinging against the underside of the fenders. Jake always drove too fast, but then, so did she.

And then she saw it. Her chin crumpled. The tip of her nose turned bright pink, and tears began to leak through the navy blue hedge of her eyelashes.

Jake, who'd been watching anxiously for her reaction, began to swear. "God, don't tell me. Marching bands, airplanes, buses . . . and yellow houses, right?"

"It's so b-b-beatiful," she wailed. Clutching his right arm, she fanned her wet lashes to clear her vision and

gazed at him as if he were Santa Claus and Clint Black all
rolled into one magnificent package. "Jake, how did you
know? I mean, why? And the sign and all..."

She almost thought he was blushing, but it had to be her
mascara clouding up her vision again, because grown men
didn't blush. Especially not men like Jake Spencer, who
were all gristle and rawhide. She blinked, sniffed and
smeared a streak of navy blue across her cheek, then tried
to wipe it off her arm between the bangles with a little bitty
lace-edged handkerchief, which her mama had always
preferred over tissues, and she did, too. At least they'd had
that much in common.

"You like it? You don't think it's too gaudy?"

She laughed, squeezing out a few more mascara-stained
tears. "Honestly, Jake, do you think anything's too gaudy
for me? I like gaudy. I *adore* gaudy. Plain is so boring."

The house was the color of scrambled eggs, the shutters
a dark, boxwood green with the panels picked out in a
paler shade. It reminded her of new growth on an old ev-
ergreen. The front door, the swing and the table she'd
dragged outside were all painted salsa red.

"I thought maybe a few bushes and things might set it
off, but down at the plant store, they said I'd do better to
wait a few months if I wanted them to live."

Jake pulled under the shed roof, out of the sun. Together, they sat and admired the house for several com-
panionable minutes. Jake thought it stuck out like a sore
thumb. Priss thought that with a little landscaping, it
would be fit for a spread in *Southern Living*.

"You really like it?" he asked hesitantly, and she started
to tear up again because her insides were too full for her
outside.

"I really like it," she whispered. "Oh, Lordy, I wish I
wasn't allergic to waterproof mascara. I can't wear bottle

tans, either. They make me itch, and you don't even want to know what mangoes do to the skin around my mouth.''

Jake wasn't exactly sure what she was talking about, but then, that was nothing new. She'd said that sometimes she went off somewhere inside her head. He reckoned he was just going to have to learn to follow her there. Either that or go quietly crazy trying to figure out where she was coming from.

''I haven't done much to the inside yet,'' he said, opening his door and easing his long legs out. He hadn't had much time for the roan stud lately, he'd been working so damned hard to get the house finished, but ladder work was tough on legs that had been busted a few too many times. Almost as tough as rodeoing.

The inside was cold as January, with the air conditioner roaring full-blast. The gray floor was still gray, the parlor furniture still as grim as ever. But there was a new feeling about the house. Priss put it down as cautiously optimistic. She peered into every room, her mind swiftly rearranging furniture, painting walls, upholstering this, replacing that. Peach, she was thinking, but then, trying to picture Jake against a peach-colored background, she settled for celery green.

''That fireplace—'' she was saying when he took her by the arm and led her back out into the hall, toward the stairs.

''Later. First, see what you think about upstairs.''

Her breath caught somewhere in the vicinity of her squash blossom necklace. Air-conditioning or not, she suddenly felt warm all over.

The upstairs hall was as dismal as ever, with the same gray floors, dingy white walls and curtainless dormers. Instead of stopping at the first door, Jake led her to the southeast corner room, which was his.

With one big, callused hand on the doorknob, he hesitated. "Priss—honey. Maybe I'm jumping the gun. I figured—that is, I thought maybe—what I'm getting at is, if you aren't interested, why then, all you have to do is say so, and I'll drive you straight back to town."

He was sweating. He took off his hat and held it over his heart. His hair needed another trim, and the mark of his hatband was clearly visible on his high, broad forehead. Already there was a shadow of stubble on his square jaw, but it was the look in his eyes that purely made her heart turn over in her breast.

"Jake, are you fixin' to take me to bed again?"

Even as she watched, his pale gray eyes turned black as sin. He lowered his hat from his chest to the front of his jeans, which she recognized as his best ones, which were slightly less faded than the rest.

"I'm most sincerely hoping to."

"Is this what you wanted to talk to me about?"

"Part of it. Yeah, I reckon so, but it's not the most important thing on my mind."

Her eyes widened. They were standing toe to toe, yet not touching. Priss could feel his heat, smell the faint aroma of laundry soap, musk and horse that was so much a part of him. "It's not?"

"No, it's not. Now, listen—I've got it all laid out in my mind what I want to say, but if you keep on interrupting me, I'm gonna get all screwed up and make a mess of it." He lifted his brows as if to offer her one last chance to speak or forever hold her peace.

She had to speak. If he was leading up to what she suspected he was leading up to, it was only fair. "Jake, before you say anything else, I need to tell you something."

A look of pain crossed his face and was gone so quickly she thought she might have imagined it. "I reckon maybe

I jumped the gun, huh? Sorry. I'll drive you back to town.''

"No, wait! I mean, not that I hold you responsible—at least, not entirely—but Jake, I'm going to have a baby.''

All the color drained right out of his face, leaving him pale as putty. ''A baby. You're going to—? You and that damned *sperm bank?*''

He sounded almost incoherent. Priss reached for his hand and began to chaff it between hers, in case he was feeling faint. ''Not me and the sperm bank. I was planning to, but it turned out that I didn't need to, because...''

"Because?'' His eyes bored into hers like a pair of stainless steel drill bits.

"Well, because I already was. Pregnant, that is. So I didn't need to—''

"It's mine,'' Jake said wonderingly. ''You're going to have my baby!''

Wordlessly, Priss nodded. She couldn't have spoken if her life depended on it.

"Judas priest, I'm going to be a daddy.'' He was grinning from ear to ear, but his voice sounded hushed, almost reverent. And then he sobered. ''Well. Okay, then. Here goes.'' Clearing his throat, he launched into a speech that was plainly rehearsed. ''First off, I've got right much money put by from sales and all. I was planning to use most of it adding onto the horse barn, but if you've got some other ideas, like maybe a baby's room, why then, that's all right, too. Second thing is, I don't drink a whole lot anymore, but now and again, I might like to cut loose some. I've never lifted a hand against a woman—never will, and I don't believe in running around once a man settles on his permanent woman. There's some that think that's sort of old-fashioned, but it makes sense to me.''

Jake looked self-conscious and magnificent all at the same time. Priss felt as if she were melting right down into her boots.

"Where was I? Oh, yeah. I don't go to church, but I don't reckon I'd mind if you was to want to start up."

"Jake—"

"About children. I never figured on having 'em, so I don't know much about this daddy-ing business, but I can learn."

"Jake—"

"What I'm trying to say is, if you're fixing to have a baby, why then, I'm going to be about the best dad-blamed daddy any kid ever had. What's more, even if it turns out you're not increasing, I still want to marry you. We could try some more. Maybe just to be certain, we'd better—"

"Jake?"

He cleared his throat, lifted his hat and settled it back on his head. "There. I think that about covers everything."

"Oh, Jake," Priss said with a sigh. She, who never wept, was weeping again. He hadn't said a word about love. He didn't have to. She knew love when she saw it.

And then he threw open the bedroom door and she commenced to laugh, but even then, it was a weepy, gasping, tearsome kind of laughter that was purely an overflowing of joy.

"I guess I should've asked you before I started fixing it up," Jake said, and she shook her head.

"It's wonderful. It's beautiful. Jake, it's the prettiest room I ever saw, only how did you know what I liked?"

"Faith said pink. Sue Ellen down at the diner said you liked a roof over your bed and you might like one of those French settees to lie back on and read in the afternoon."

The walls were the color of strawberry ice cream. The floors were carpeted in rose, patterned with what appeared to be watermelon vines. The chaise longue was dark green velvet to match the painted and decorated chest of drawers and the velvet draperies at the tall, ripple-glass windows. There was a lot of ruffly white eyelet embroidery all over the windows, too—and the vanity and the king-size canopied bed.

It was wonderfully gaudy. It was Nora Barrington's worst nightmare and Priss's dream come true, mostly because of the big, rawhide man who stood in the middle of the room, watching her with an aching look of uncertainty on his rugged face.

But partly, too, because she truly did like gaudy.

"If you don't like it, you can scrap it and start all over again. I can afford it."

"It's beautiful," she said with a sigh. "Jake, I love it. And oh, how I do love you."

Later, she never knew which one of them made the first move. She did recall mentioning that she liked soft mattresses, and Jake said something about feather beds, but by the time they made it to the bed, both were naked and neither one of them was thinking much about furniture.

"God, I missed you," he said with a groan as he lowered himself stiffly onto the mattress, which wasn't awfully soft, not that either of them noticed. "A dozen times I got nearly to town and then lost my nerve."

"I kept trying so hard to forget you, but the more I tried, the more I thought about what it was I was trying so hard to forget."

"You've got the most beautiful body in the world," he said reverently, touching her breasts, which she fancied were already slightly fuller, and then sliding his hand down to her belly, which wasn't, but soon would be.

They would talk more about the baby, she thought, but not now. Oh, my mercy, no—not when he was touching her the way he was, and doing all those wonderfully wicked things to her with his hands and his tongue.

When she rose to her knees and began to return the favor, Jake braced himself, gripping the pink-and-green flowered sheets with both hands. If she had the least notion of what she was doing to him, he would never be able to call his soul his own.

Couldn't anyhow. When a man went down as hard as he had, he was truly down for the count.

He was too hungry for her to wait a moment longer. Handling her as gently as if she might break, he turned her over onto her back and knelt over her. "Stop me if I get too rough," he said huskily. The fire that burned deep in his eyes was reflected in hers.

"Jake, I'm going to have a baby. That doesn't mean I'm an invalid. *Please* . . . " Her breath caught in her throat as he thrust inside her. Light seemed to splinter around her head, and then she closed her eyes and let it happen.

And happen, it did. If the first time had been almost wonderful, the second time was all the superlatives in the world. There simply were no words to describe what was happening to her as Jake drove into her body again and again, his teeth clenched, his eyes closed, a look of exquisite agony on his sharp-planed face.

With a sharp cry, Jake collapsed on top of her, but almost immediately he rolled over onto his side, drawing her with him. Cradling her in his arms, he slept.

For a long time, Priss stayed awake, thinking of what they had just shared—thinking of what she had so nearly missed. If Jake hadn't happened into the Baby Boutique—if she hadn't been in there, too—or if he had found what he wanted and left before they could meet . . .

No. God wouldn't be so cruel.

She slept for a while, safe and secure in the arms of love. It was pitch dark when she awoke, to find that Jake was awake, too.

"I reckon we got carried away," he murmured.

His voice rippled over her, raising goose bumps. "I reckon we did," she whispered.

"I don't reckon we'd better do it again today, what with you being in the family way and all. Once a day is probably okay, though, don't you think?"

"I take vitamins."

"Oh."

Playfully, Priss swung one leg over Jake's hips. "Maybe you'd better start taking them, too." She could tell from the way he was sucking his breath in between his teeth in teensy little gasps that he wasn't quite as relaxed as he was pretending to be.

"You know, I've been thinking about Pete and Rosalie," she mused.

The fact that she was able to think at all put her one up on Jake. Literally, as it happened. "Yeah?" he said between clenched teeth as she settled into position athwart his hips.

"I mean, what are we going to do if they don't get along?"

He groaned. He could see right now that it was going to be a long night. A long fifty-odd years, if he survived it. "I reckon they can stake out their separate territories, mark 'em, and try not to step on the boundaries," he said. "Me, I've already staked out mine."

Gazing down at him from her lofty position, her streaky blond hair tumbling over her freckled shoulders, Priss said gravely, "I didn't ask if you minded. About me being— um, where I am." She jiggled her hips on his thighs as if to

demonstrate. "There was this article I read about variety
that said—"

Jake closed his eyes and prayed for endurance. "I gotta
find out where you're gettin' all this readin' material.
Honey, why do you think I call this place the Bar Nothing?" he asked.

Priss looked startled. And then she began to laugh.

And then Jake did, too.

And then, for a long, long time, neither one of them had
very much to say.

* * * * *

*Don't miss the next book
in Silhouette's exciting
DADDY KNOWS LAST series.*

Here's a sneak preview of

BABY IN A BASKET

*by Helen R. Meyers
available in August from
Silhouette Romance.*

Baby in a Basket

"What a difference a day makes, eh, folks? It's Monday, August 17. Stay right here at KDYL for breaking news about the approaching line of thunder—"

Mitch McCord shut off the radio. He didn't need to hear anything about the weather. A different, more catastrophic storm had already exploded right over his head, and the National Weather Service would be of no use to him whatsoever. But one thing was worth noting: twenty-four hours could make an incredible difference in a person's life.

Amazing. Yesterday at this very moment he'd been climbing to thirty thousand feet on his way to California. Today he was sitting here on his driveway, trying to sum up the courage to go next door and face his future.

"This is your life, Captain Mitchell Sean McCord. Do not pass Go, do not collect two hundred dollars. Just get your butt out of this ego machine, and watch what the bluebird of happiness bequeaths *you.*"

To think he used to believe being grounded was the worst thing that could ever happen to him. Short of utter disaster in the sky, that is—but he worked hard not to dwell on such a thing. He was a man who stayed in control, the guy who made things happen. A participant, not an observer. Well, apparently he'd participated one time too many. Where was his infamous power of positive thinking now?

Hang gliding in the Twilight Zone.

Too true. And it did no good to sit and mope. It certainly wouldn't resolve his dilemma. Ready or not, he had to go knock at Jenny Stevens's door and say, "Hey, Jen. Guess I'd better take the baby. My daughter. The one left on my doorstep this morning. With a note saying 'Take care of *your* child.'"

A movement out of the corner of his eye had Mitch looking toward the right where Jenny peered out at him from the lacy-curtained frame that was her kitchen window. Ever-observant Jenny. Heaven only knew what she must think of him at this point.

With a heavy sigh, he shoved open the door and climbed out of the sports car. There was no putting this off. If he didn't go in, she would come out. The smartest thing would be to meet her on her turf, pronounce the verdict, and beg for help. *More* help, since she'd already been wonderful that morning. Of course, he already knew what she was going to say. After living next to her for nearly half his life, he doubted Saint Jenny could surprise him much.

She would be supportive, sweetly reassuring, and generous to a suffocating fault. Agony. Nevertheless, he needed that right now—at least until he could figure out what to do about this mess.

He crossed from his property to hers, and approached the small house constructed of pink and gray granite with a white curlicue sign out front noting Jams By Jenny.

Surely he could converse with one harmless female for a few minutes and come away with what he wanted?

He almost had himself convinced. Then she opened the door and laughed at him.

"Well, for pity's sake, McCord. You look like the verdict's death by hanging."

Apparently nothing was going to go as expected today. Mitch shot her a sour look. "It might as well be."

Jenny's dark eyes went wide and she clasped her hands together. "She's yours, then? I mean, of course she's yours. Anyone who looks at that baby would know it in a heartbeat. But... there's been no missing persons bulletin filed? No call by a bereft mother? What did they say at the police station? Did you stop by the hospital, as I suggested?"

Since when did the woman prattle like a teenager with her first telephone? "Let me know when it's my turn to say something."

He knew he sounded like a grump, but he simply couldn't help himself. Who needed all that bubbly chatter? Or the evocative scent of fresh baked muffins that attacked him as she stepped aside and he entered her kitchen!

There was no sound coming from across the room where the baby lay. This triggered Mitch's curiosity, as well as a smattering of hope. If the kid wasn't hungry at this point, Mitch told himself, he had a chance left yet, because no kid of *his* could be around aromas like this without ending up with a growling stomach.

Suddenly a pitiful wail erupted from the woven hamper on the kitchen table. Mitch hung his head. So there it was, the final knockout punch—as if he needed one at this point.

The exciting new cross-line continuity series about love, marriage—and Daddy's unexpected need for a baby carriage!

It all began with *THE BABY NOTION*
by Dixie Browning (Desire #1011 7/96)

And the romance in New Hope, Texas, continues with:

BABY IN A BASKET
by Helen R. Myers (Romance #1169 8/96)

Confirmed bachelor Mitch McCord finds a baby on
his doorstep and turns to lovely gal-next-door
Jenny Stevens for some lessons in fatherhood—and love!

Don't miss the upcoming books in this wonderful series:

MARRIED...WITH TWINS!
by Jennifer Mikels (Special Edition #1054, 9/96)

HOW TO HOOK A HUSBAND (AND A BABY)
by Carolyn Zane (Yours Truly #29, 10/96)

DISCOVERED: DADDY
by Marilyn Pappano (Intimate Moments #746, 11/96)

DADDY KNOWS LAST continues
each month...only from

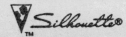

Look us up on-line at: http://www.romance.net

DKL-R

FORTUNE'S Children™

New York Times Bestselling Author
REBECCA
BRANDEWYNE

Launches a new twelve-book series—FORTUNE'S CHILDREN
beginning in July 1996 with Book One

Hired Husband

Caroline Fortune knew her marriage to Nick Valkov was in
name only. She would help save the family business, Nick
would get a green card, and a paper marriage would suit both
of them. Until Caroline could no longer deny the feelings Nick
stirred in her and the practical union turned passionate.

MEET THE FORTUNES—a family whose legacy is greater than
riches. Because where there's a will...there's a wedding!

Look for Book Two, *The Millionaire and the Cowgirl*,
by Lisa Jackson. Available in August 1996 wherever Silhouette
books are sold.

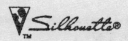

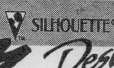